W9-CHJ-114

THE HUMAN COMEDY

WILLIAM SAROYAN

The Human
Comedy

ILLUSTRATED BY DON FREEMAN

EDITED BY MARION C. SHERIDAN

HEAD OF THE ENGLISH DEPARTMENT, NEW HAVEN HIGH SCHOOL

HARCOURT BRACE JOVANOVICH, PUBLISHERS

NEW YORK   CHICAGO   SAN FRANCISCO   ATLANTA

DALLAS   *and*   LONDON

COPYRIGHT 1943, BY

WILLIAM SAROYAN

COPYRIGHT © 1944 BY

HARCOURT BRACE JOVANOVICH, INC.

All rights reserved. No part of this publication may be reproduced or trans-
mitted in any form or by any means, electronic or mechanical, including
photocopy, recording, or any information storage and retrieval system,
without permission in writing from the pubilsher.

ISBN:0-15-347223-5

PRINTED IN THE UNITED STATES OF AMERICA

Before you read The Human Comedy

*And to love comedy you must know
the real world, and know men and women
well enough not to expect too much of
them, though you may still hope for
good.* — GEORGE MEREDITH

The Human Comedy makes a direct appeal to people of all ages, who read with enjoyment of Homer Macauley, the telegraph messenger; Ulysses, his four-year old brother; their mother; their sister, Bess; their brother, Marcus, in the Army; and their father, Matthew, who died before the book opened, — but who still lives.

The story is a simple one of family life in a small ordinary community, part of the "strange, weed-infested, junky, wonderful, senseless yet beautiful world" of which William Saroyan writes. Work experiences, with which the author was familiar, lead into the joys and griefs of all parts of the town. War experiences carry the story away from and back to the home in Ithaca.

In his dedication Mr. Saroyan tells his mother, Takoohi Saroyan, that he has written the story, which is for her, as simply as possible. The words are simple, natural, and familiar. Most of the sentences are brief. The book itself, the author's first novel, is short. The author has an artist's power, a poet's power, of saying much in a few commonplace words that take on new meaning. He omits details that merely describe, using those that reveal. By the happy choice of a few telling items he draws a picture that has a strange way of recalling past events and emotions.

The characters are human and lovable. Many are children, or the so-called unfortunate, or people of foreign extraction, possibly Armenians, familiar to Mr. Saroyan through his own ancestry. And the characters are men and women from whom you do not expect too much, "though you may still hope for good." All are treated with sympathy, understanding and a kindly gentle humor that does not provoke uproarious mirth but rather "laughs through the mind."

Mr. Saroyan knows something of California, where he was born in 1908, the youngest of four children. When William was two, his father died. For the next five years William was in an orphanage in Alameda, California, where he may have met boys like Tobey George, who didn't know about parents until he went to school. When William was seven, his mother, Takoohi, for whom he reveals his affection and his admiration in the dedication, went to work in a cannery, and the family returned to Fresno. He has deep family pride.

Reading widely, William went as far as the second year of junior high school. It has been said that at three he started to write. At fifteen he had a typewriter. As a boy he sold newspapers and probably learned just how to fold them, by whacking and a magician's trick. After leaving school, he went to work as a telegraph messenger. Later he was the local manager of the Postal Telegraph office in San Francisco. From experience he knows that telegrams touch the lives of people at crises. In *My Name Is Aram* he tells in an indirect way of the years from seven to seventeen (1915 to 1925). At seventeen he left his native valley.

Since then Mr. Saroyan has traveled to various parts of America as well as to Armenia, Russia, and Ireland. He has had more than five hundred short stories published and many plays presented. An original radio play is called "Special Announcement."

Reversing the usual order, Mr. Saroyan wrote *The Human Comedy,* his first full-length novel, as a motion picture and then as a novel. Almost simultaneously both were outstanding: the novel was the choice of the Book-of-the-Month Club; the motion picture was second in popularity only to "The Watch on the Rhine."

Mr. Saroyan must have delighted in naming the book *The Human Comedy,* a slender book about people for the most part in one small place in a Western state. The title was not original, for one hundred years ago a French writer, Balzac, wrote at length, book after book, in his endeavor to reveal all mankind in *The Human Comedy.*

It is really unimportant whether the title is grandiloquent or flippant or reverent or ironical or serious. The author sees beyond the conventional and the lifeless. He was indifferent to definitions of short stories or novels or plays. He wanted writing to "breathe," and unquestionably *The Human Comedy* breathes.

Novels reveal life; they pulse with life. This intimate, homely, pretentious and unpretentious book reveals life; playfully and profoundly it touches upon **the** human scene.

This Story is for
TAKOOHI SAROYAN

*I have taken all this time to write a story especially for
you because I have wanted it to be an especially good
story, the very best I might ever be able to write, and
now at last, a little pressed for time, I have tried. I might
have waited longer still, but as there is no telling what's
next or what skill or inclination will be left after everything else, I have hurried a little and taken a chance on
my present skill and inclination. Soon, I hope, someone
wonderful will translate the story into Armenian, so that
it will be in print you know well. In translation the story
may read better than it does in English, and, as you have
done before, maybe you will want to read some of it to
me, even though I wrote the stuff in the first place. If so,
I promise to listen, and to marvel at the beauty of our
language, so little known by others and so much less ap-
preciated by anyone than by you. As you cannot read
and enjoy English as well as you read and enjoy Armenian, and as I cannot read or write Armenian at all,
we can only hope for a good translator. One way or
another, though, this story is for you. I hope you like it.
I have written it as simply as possible, with that blend-
ing of the severe and the light-hearted which is especially
yours, and our family's. The story is not enough, I know,
but what of that? It will surely seem enough to you,
since your son wrote it and meant so well.*

W. S.

CONTENTS

Contents

Contents

The Human Comedy

CHAPTER 1

ULYSSES

The little boy named Ulysses Macauley one day stood over the new gopher hole in the backyard of his house on Santa Clara Avenue in Ithaca, California. The gopher of this hole pushed up fresh moist dirt and peeked out at the boy, who was certainly a stranger but perhaps not an enemy. Before this miracle had been fully enjoyed by the boy, one of the birds of Ithaca flew into the old walnut tree in the backyard and after settling itself on a branch broke into rapture, moving the boy's fascination from the earth to the tree. Next, best of all, a freight train puffed and roared far away. The boy listened,

3

and felt the earth beneath him tremble with the moving of the train. Then he broke into running, moving (it seemed to him) swifter than any life in the world.

When he reached the crossing he was just in time to see the passing of the whole train, from locomotive to caboose. He waved to the engineer, but the engineer did not wave back to him. He waved to five others who were with the train, but not one of them waved back. They might have done so, but they didn't. At last a Negro appeared leaning over the side of a gondola. Above the clatter of the train, Ulysses heard the man singing:

"Weep no more, my lady, O weep no more today
We will sing one song for the old Kentucky home
For the old Kentucky home far away"

Ulysses waved to the Negro too, and then a wondrous and unexpected thing happened. *This* man, black and different from all the others, waved back to Ulysses, shouting: "Going home, boy—going back where I belong!"

The small boy and the Negro waved to one another until the train was almost out of sight.

Then Ulysses looked around. There it was, all around him, funny and lonely—the world of his life. The strange, weed-infested, junky, wonderful, senseless yet beautiful world. Walking down the track came an old man with a rolled bundle on his back. Ulysses waved to this man too. but the man was too old and too tired to be pleased with a small boy's friendliness. The old man glanced at Ulysses as if both he and the boy were already dead.

The little boy turned slowly and started for home. As he moved, he still listened to the passing of the train, the singing of the Negro, and the joyous words: "Going home, boy—going back where I belong!" He stopped to think of all this, loitering beside a china-ball tree and kicking at the yellow, smelly, fallen fruit of it. After a moment he smiled the smile of the Macauley people—the gentle, wise, secret smile which said *Yes* to all things.

When he turned the corner and saw the Macauley house, Ulysses began to skip, kicking up a heel. He tripped and fell because of this merriment, but got to his feet and went on.

His mother was in the yard, throwing feed to the chickens. She watched the boy trip and fall and get up and skip again. He came quickly and quietly and stood beside her, then went to the hen nest to look for eggs. He found one. He looked at it a moment, picked it up, brought it to his mother and very carefully handed it to her, by which he meant what no man can guess and no child can remember to tell.

CHAPTER 2

HOMER

His brother Homer sat on the seat of a second-hand bicycle which struggled bravely with the dirt of a country road. Homer Macauley wore a telegraph messenger's coat which was far too big and a cap which was not quite big enough. The sun was going down in a somnolence of evening peace deeply cherished by the people of Ithaca. All about the messenger orchards and vineyards rested in the old, old earth of California. Even though he was moving along swiftly, Homer was not missing any of the charm of the region. Look at that! he kept saying to himself of earth and tree, sun and grass and cloud.

Look at that, will you? He began to make decorations with the movements of his bike and, to accompany these ornaments of movement, he burst out with a shouting of music—simple, lyrical and ridiculous. The theme of this opera was taken over in his mind by the strings of an orchestra, then supplemented by the harp of his mother and the piano of his sister Bess. And finally, to bring the whole family together, an accordion came into the group, saying the music with a smiling and somber sweetness, as Homer remembered his brother Marcus.

Homer's music fled before the hurrying clatter of three incredible objects moving across the sky. The messenger looked up at these objects, and promptly rode into a small dry ditch. Airplanes, Homer said to himself. A farmer's dog came swiftly and with great importance, barking like a man with a message. Homer ignored the message, turning only once to spoof the animal by saying "Arp, Arp!" He seated himself on the bicycle again and rode on.

When he reached the beginning of the residential district of the city, he passed a sign without reading it:

ITHACA, CALIFORNIA

EAST, WEST—HOME IS BEST

WELCOME, STRANGER

He stopped at the next corner to behold a long line of Army trucks full of soldiers roll by. He saluted the men, just as his brother Ulysses had waved to the engineer and the hoboes. A great many soldiers returned the messenger's salute. Why not? What did they know about anything?

CHAPTER 3

THE TELEGRAPH OFFICE

It was evening in Ithaca when Homer finally drew up in front of the telegraph office. The clock in the window said two minutes past seven. Inside the office Homer saw Mr. Spangler, the manager of the telegraph office, counting the words of a telegram which a tired-looking, troubled young man of twenty or so had just handed him. As he came into the office, Homer listened to Mr. Spangler and the young man.

"Fourteen words collect," Spangler said. He paused a moment, glancing at the boy. "Little short of money?"

The boy couldn't reply immediately, but soon he said, "Yes, sir. A little.—But my mother will send me enough to get home on."

"Sure," Spangler said. "Where you been?"

"Nowhere, I guess," the boy said, and began to cough. "How long will it take the telegram to get to my mother?"

"Well," Spangler said, "it's pretty late in the East now. It's not easy to raise money late at night sometimes, but I'll rush the telegram right through." Without looking at the boy again, Spangler went through his pockets, coming out with a handful of small coins, one piece of currency and a hard-boiled egg.

"Here," he said, "just in case." He handed the boy the currency. "You can pay me back when your mother sends the money," he said. He indicated the egg. "I picked it up in a bar seven days ago. Brings me luck."

The boy looked at the money. "What's this?" he said.

"It's nothing," Spangler said.

"Thanks," the boy said. He stopped, amazed and embarrassed. "Thanks," he said again, and hurried out of the office.

Spangler took the telegram over to William Grogan, the night-shift telegraph operator and wire-chief. "Send it paid, Willie," he said. "I'll pay for it myself."

The Telegraph Office

Mr. Grogan put his hand around the "bug" and began rattling off the telegram, letter by letter:

MRS. MARGARET STRICKMAN
1874 BIDDLE STREET
YORK, PENNSYLVANIA

DEAR MA. PLEASE TELEGRAPH THIRTY DOLLARS. WANT TO COME HOME. AM FINE. EVERYTHING O.K.

JOHN

Homer Macauley studied the delivery desk to see what was on hand for delivery, or if there were any calls to take. Mr. Spangler watched him with dead-pan fascination, and then spoke to him.

"How do you like being a messenger?" he said.

"How do I *like* it?" Homer said. "I like it better than anything. You sure get to see a lot of different people. You sure get to go to a lot of different places."

"Yeah," Spangler said. He paused to look at the boy a little closer. "How did you sleep last night?"

"Fine," Homer said. "I was pretty tired but I slept fine."

"Did you sleep a little at school today?"

"A little."

"What subject?"

"Ancient history."

"What about sports?" Spangler said. "I mean what about not being able to take part in them on account of having this job?"

"I take part in them," Homer said. "We have a physical education period every day."

"Is that so?" Spangler said. "I used to run the two-twenty low hurdles when I went to Ithaca High. Valley Champion." The manager of the telegraph office paused, then went on. "You really like this job, don't you?"

"I'm going to be the best messenger this office ever had," Homer said.

"O.K.," Spangler said. "Just don't kill yourself—don't go too fast. Get there swiftly, but don't go *too* fast. Be polite to everybody—take your hat off in elevators, and above all things don't lose a telegram."

"Yes, sir."

"Working nights is different from working days," Spangler went on. "Taking a telegram to Chinatown or out to the sticks is liable to scare a fellow—well, don't let it scare *you*. People are people. Don't be scared of them. How old are you?"

Homer gulped. "Sixteen," he said.

"Yeah, I know," Spangler said. "You said that yesterday. We're not supposed to hire a boy unless he's at least sixteen, but I thought I'd take a chance on you. How old are you?"

"Fourteen," Homer said.

"Well," Spangler said, "you'll be sixteen in two years."

"Yes, sir," Homer said.

"If anything comes up that you don't understand," Spangler said, "come to me."

"Yes, sir," Homer said. He paused. "What about singing telegrams?"

"Nothing to them," Spangler said. "We don't get many of them. You've got a pretty good voice, haven't you?"

"I used to sing at the First Presbyterian Sunday School of Ithaca," Homer said.

"That's fine," Spangler said. "That's exactly the kind of voice we need for our singing telegrams. Now let's say Mr. Grogan over there was sent a birthday greeting. How would you do it?"

Homer went over to Mr. Grogan and sang:

"Happy birthday to you—
Happy birthday to you—
Happy birthday, dear Grogan—
Happy birthday to you."

"Thank you," Mr. Grogan said.

"That's fine," Spangler said to Homer, "but you wouldn't say 'dear Grogan,' you'd say 'dear *Mr.* Grogan.' What are you going to do with the fifteen dollars a week?"

"Give it to my mother," Homer said.

"All right," Spangler said. "From now on you're working—*steady*. You're part of this outfit. Watch things—listen carefully—keep your eyes and ears open." The manager of the telegraph office looked away at nothing a moment and then said, "What future have you mapped out for yourself?"

"Future?" Homer said. He was a little embarrassed because all his life, from day to day, he had been busy mapping out a future, even if it was only a future for the next day. "Well," he said, "I don't know for sure, but I guess I'd like to be somebody some day. Maybe a composer or somebody like that —some day."

"That's fine," Spangler said, "and this is the place to start. Music all around you—real music—straight from the world—straight from the hearts of people. Hear those telegraph keys? Beautiful music."

"Yes, sir," Homer said.

Spangler asked suddenly, "You know where Chatterton's Bakery is on Broadway? Here's a quarter. Go get me two day-old pies—apple and cocoanut cream. Two for a quarter."

"Yes, sir," Homer said. He caught the quarter Spangler tossed to him and ran out of the office. Spangler looked after him, moving along into idle, pleasant, nostalgic dreaming. When he came out of the dream, he turned to the telegraph operator and said, "What do you think of him?"

"He's a good boy," Mr. Grogan said.

"*I* think he is," Spangler said. "Comes from a good, poor family on Santa Clara Avenue. No father. Brother in the Army. Mother works in the packinghouses in the summer. Sister goes to State College. He's a couple of years underage, that's all."

"I'm a couple overage," Mr. Grogan said. "We'll get along."

Spangler got up from his desk. "If you want me,"

he said, "I'll be at Corbett's. Share the pies between you—" He stopped and stared, dumbfounded, as Homer came running into the office with two wrapped-up pies.

"What's your name again?" Spangler almost shouted at the boy.

"Homer Macauley," Homer said.

The manager of the telegraph office put his arm around the new messenger. "All right, Homer Macauley," he said. "You're the boy this office needs on the night-shift. You're probably the fastest-moving thing in the San Joaquin valley. You're going to be a great man some day, too—if you live. So see that you live." He turned and left the office while Homer tried to understand the meaning of what the man had said.

"All right, boy," Mr. Grogan said, "the pies."

Homer put the pies on the desk beside Mr. Grogan, who continued to talk. "Homer Macauley," he said, "my name is William Grogan. I am called Willie, however, although I am sixty-seven years old. I am an old-time telegrapher, one of the last in the world. I am also night wire-chief of this office. I am also a man who has memories of many wondrous worlds gone by. I am also hungry. Let us feast together on these pies—the apple and the cocoanut cream. From now on, you and I are friends."

"Yes, sir," Homer said.

The old telegraph operator broke one of the pies

into four parts, and they began to eat cocoanut cream.

"I shall, on occasion," Mr. Grogan said, "ask you to run an errand for me, to join me in song, or to sit and talk to me. In the event of drunkenness, I shall expect of you a depth of understanding one may not expect from men past twelve. How old are you?"

"Fourteen," Homer said, "but I guess I've got a pretty good understanding."

"Very well," Mr. Grogan said. "I'll take your word for it. Every night in this office I shall count on you to see that I shall be able to perform my duties. A splash of cold water in the face if I do not respond when shaken—this is to be followed by a cup of hot black coffee from Corbett's."

"Yes, sir," Homer said.

"On the street, however," Mr. Grogan continued, "the procedure is quite another thing. If you behold me wrapped in the embrace of alcohol, greet me as you pass, but make no reference to my happiness. I am a sensitive man and prefer not to be the object of public solicitude."

"Cold water and coffee in the office," Homer said. "Greeting in the street. Yes, sir."

Mr. Grogan went on, his mouth full of cocoanut cream. "Do you feel this world is going to be a better place after the War?"

Homer thought a moment and then said, "Yes, sir."

"Do you like cocoanut cream?" Mr. Grogan said.

The Telegraph Office

"Yes, sir," Homer said.

The telegraph box rattled. Mr. Grogan answered the call and took his place at the typewriter, but went on talking. "I, too, am fond of cocoanut cream," he said. "Also music, especially singing. I believe I overheard you say that once upon a time you sang at Sunday School. Please be good enough to sing one of the Sunday School songs while I type this message from Washington, D. C."

Homer sang *Rock of Ages* while Mr. Grogan typed the telegram. It was addressed to Mrs. Rosa Sandoval, 1129 G Street, Ithaca, California, and in the telegram the War Department informed Mrs. Sandoval that her son, Juan Domingo Sandoval, had been killed in action.

Mr. Grogan handed the message to Homer. He then took a long drink from the bottle he kept in the drawer beside his chair. Homer folded the telegram, put it in an envelope, sealed the envelope, put the envelope in his cap and left the office. When the messenger was gone, the old telegraph operator lifted his voice, singing *Rock of Ages*. For once upon a time he too had been as young as any man.

CHAPTER 4

ALL THE WORLD WILL BE JEALOUS OF ME

Music came from the Macauley house on Santa Clara Avenue. Bess and Mrs. Macauley played *All the World Will Be Jealous of Me*. They played the song for the soldier Marcus, wherever he happened to be, because it was the song he loved most. Mary Arena came into the parlor from the house next door, stood beside Bess at the piano and soon began to sing. She sang for Marcus, who was all the world to *her*. The small boy Ulysses listened and watched. Something was mysterious somewhere and he wanted to find out what it was, even though he was half asleep. At last he summoned enough energy to say:

"Where's Marcus?"

Mrs. Macauley looked at the boy.

"You must try to understand," she began to say, then stopped.

Ulysses tried to understand but didn't know just what was to be understood.

"Understand what?" he said.

"Marcus," Mrs. Macauley said, "has gone away from Ithaca."

"Why?" Ulysses said.

"Marcus is in the Army," Mrs. Macauley said.

"When is he coming home?" the little boy said.

"When the War is over," Mrs. Macauley said.

"Tomorrow?"

"No, not tomorrow."

"When?"

"We don't know. We're waiting."

"Then where is my father?" Ulysses said. "If we wait, will *he* come home like Marcus too?"

"No," Mrs. Macauley said, "not that way. He will not come walking down the street, up the steps, across the porch, and on into the house, as he used to do."

This too was too much for the boy, and as there was only one word with which to hope for something like truth and comfort, he said this word:

"Why?"

Mrs. Macauley turned to Bess and Mary.

"Death," she said, "is not an easy thing for anyone to understand, least of all a child, but every life shall one day end." She looked now at Ulysses. "That day came for your father two years ago." She looked back at Bess and Mary. "But as long as we are alive," she said, "as long as we are together, as long as *two* of us are left, and remember him, nothing in the world can take him from us. His body can be taken, but not *him*. You shall know your father better as you grow and know yourself better," she said. "He is not dead, because *you* are alive. Time and accident, illness and weariness took his body, but already you have given it back to him, younger and more eager than ever. I don't expect you to understand anything I'm telling you. But I know you will remember *this*—that nothing good ever ends. If it did, there would be no people in the world—no life at all, anywhere. And the world is full of people and full of wonderful life."

The boy thought about this a moment and then remembered what he had witnessed earlier that day.

"What are the gophers?" he said.

His mother was not at all unprepared for such a question. She knew that he had eyes, and beyond eyes vision, and beyond vision heart and passion and love—not for one thing alone, or for one *kind* of thing, but for any and all.

"The gophers of the earth," she said, "the birds overhead, the fish in the sea are all part of the life of things—and part of *our* life. Everything alive is part of each of us, and many things which do not move as we move are part of us. The sun is part of us, the earth, the sky, the stars, the rivers, and the oceans. All things are part of us, and we have come here to enjoy them and to thank God for them."

The little boy accepted this news.

"Then where is Homer?" he said.

"Your brother Homer," Mrs. Macauley said, "is working. Yesterday he found himself a job after school. He will be home after midnight, when you are in bed asleep."

The small boy could not understand. What was work? Why was his brother working? What delight came to a man from working?

"Why is Homer working?" he said.

The two girls sat by patiently, waiting for Mrs. Macauley's answers to the child's questions.

"Your brother Homer is working," she said, "because your brother Marcus is in the Army. Because we must have money with which to buy food and clothing and pay rent—and to give to others whose need is greater than ours."

"*Who?*" Ulysses said.

"Anybody," Mrs. Macauley said. "The poor, for instance."

"Who're the poor?" the boy said.

"Everybody," Mrs. Macauley said, smiling to herself.

Ulysses tried hard to stay awake, but it was no longer possible.

"You must remember," she said, "always to give, of everything you have. You must give foolishly even. You must be extravagant. You must give to all who come into your life. Then nothing and no one shall have the power to cheat you of anything, for if you give to a thief, he cannot steal from you, and he himself is then no longer a thief. And the more you give, the more you will have to give."

Mrs. Macauley looked from the boy to his sister Bess. "Put him to bed," she said.

Bess and Mary took the boy to his room. When they were gone and she sat alone, the woman heard a footstep and turned. There at the door she saw Matthew Macauley as if he were not dead.

"I fell asleep," he said. "I was very sleepy. Please forgive me, Katey."

He laughed as if it were Ulysses laughing, and when Bess came back to the parlor she said, "He laughed just before we tucked him in."

CHAPTER 5

YOU GO YOUR WAY, I'LL GO MINE

The messenger got off his bicycle in front of the house of Mrs. Rosa Sandoval. He went to the door and knocked gently. He knew almost immediately that someone was inside the house. He could not hear anything, but he was sure the knock was bringing someone to the door and he was most eager to see who this person would be—this woman named Rosa Sandoval who was now to hear of murder in the world and to feel it in herself. The door was not a long time opening, but there was no hurry in the way it moved on its hinges. The movement of the door was as if, whoever she was, she had nothing in the world to fear. Then the door was open, and there she was.

To Homer the Mexican woman was beautiful. He could see that she had been patient all her life, so that now, after years of it, her lips were set in a gentle and saintly smile. But like all people who never receive telegrams the appearance of a messenger at the front door is full of terrible implications. Homer knew that Mrs. Rosa Sandoval was shocked to see him. Her first word was the first word of all surprise. She said "Oh," as if instead of a messenger she had thought of opening the door to someone she had known a long time and would be pleased to sit down with. Before she spoke again she studied Homer's eyes and Homer knew that she knew the message was not a welcome one.

"You have a telegram?" she said.

It wasn't Homer's fault. His work was to deliver telegrams. Even so, it seemed to him that he was part of the whole mistake. He felt awkward and almost as if he *alone* were responsible for what had happened. At the same time he wanted to come right out and say, "I'm only a messenger, Mrs. Sandoval. I'm very sorry I must bring you a telegram like this, but it is only because it is my work to do so."

"Who is it for?" the Mexican woman said.

"Mrs. Rosa Sandoval, 1129 G Street," Homer

said. He extended the telegram to the Mexican woman, but she would not touch it.

"Are you Mrs. Sandoval?" Homer said.

"Please," the woman said. "Please come in. I cannot read English. I am Mexican. I read only *La Prensa* which comes from Mexico City." She paused a moment and looked at the boy standing awkwardly as near the door as he could be and still be inside the house.

"Please," she said, "what does the telegram say?"

"Mrs. Sandoval," the messenger said, "the telegram says—"

But now the woman interrupted him. "But you must *open* the telegram and *read* it to me," she said. "You have not opened it."

"Yes, ma'am," Homer said as if he were speaking to a school teacher who had just corrected him.

He opened the telegram with nervous fingers. The Mexican woman stooped to pick up the torn envelope, and tried to smooth it out. As she did so she said, "Who sent the telegram—my son Juan Domingo?"

"No, ma'am," Homer said. "The telegram is from the War Department."

"War Department?" the Mexican woman said.

"Mrs. Sandoval," Homer said swiftly, "your son is dead. Maybe it's a mistake. Everybody makes a mistake, Mrs. Sandoval. Maybe it wasn't your son. Maybe it was somebody else. The telegram *says* it was Juan Domingo. But maybe the telegram is wrong."

The Mexican woman pretended not to hear.

"Oh, do not be afraid," she said. "Come inside. Come inside. I will bring you candy." She took the boy's arm and brought him to the table at the center of the room and there she made him sit.

"All boys like candy," she said. "I will bring you candy." She went into another room and soon returned with an old chocolate candy box. She opened the box at the table and in it Homer saw a strange kind of candy.

"Here," she said. "Eat this candy. All boys like candy."

Homer took a piece of the candy from the box, put it into his mouth, and tried to chew.

"You would not bring me a bad telegram," she said. "You are a good boy—like my little Juanito when he was a little boy. Eat another piece." And she made the messenger take another piece of the candy.

Homer sat chewing the dry candy while the Mexican woman talked. "It is our own candy," she said, "from cactus. I make it for my Juanito when he come home, but *you* eat it. You are my boy too."

Now suddenly she began to sob, holding herself in as if weeping were a disgrace. Homer wanted to get up and run but he knew he would stay. He even thought he might stay the rest of his life. He just didn't know what else to do to try to make the woman less unhappy, and if she had *asked* him to take the place of her son, he would not have been able to refuse, because he would not have known how. He got to his feet as if by standing he meant to begin correcting what could not be corrected and then he knew the foolishness of this intention and became more awkward than ever. In his heart he was saying over and over again, "What can I do? What the hell can *I* do? I'm only the messenger."

The woman suddenly took him in her arms, saying, "My little boy, my little boy!"

He didn't know why, because he only felt wounded by the whole thing, but for some reason he was sickened through all his blood and thought he would need to vomit. He didn't *dislike* the woman or anybody else, but what was happening to her seemed so wrong and so full of ugliness that he was sick and didn't know if he ever wanted to go on living again.

"Come now," the woman said. "Sit down here." She forced him into another chair and stood over him. "Let me look at you," she said. She looked at him strangely and, sick everywhere within himself, the messenger could not move. He felt neither love nor hate but something very close to disgust, but at the same time he felt great compassion, not for the poor woman alone, but for all things and the ridiculous way of their enduring and dying. He saw her back in time, a beautiful young woman sitting beside the crib of her infant son. He saw her looking down at this amazing human thing, speechless and helpless and full of the world to come. He saw her rocking the crib and he heard her singing to the child. Now look at her, he said to himself.

He was on his bicycle suddenly, riding swiftly down the dark street, tears coming out of his eyes and his mouth whispering young and crazy curses. When he got back to the telegraph office the tears had stopped, but everything else had started and he knew there would be no stopping them. "Otherwise I'm just as good as dead myself," he said, as if someone were listening whose hearing was not perfect.

CHAPTER 6

A SONG FOR MR. GROGAN

Homer sat across the table from Mr. Grogan. The telegraph wires were silent now, but suddenly the box began to rattle. Homer waited for Mr. Grogan to answer the call, but Mr. Grogan did not answer it. Homer ran around the table.

"Mr. Grogan," he said, "they're calling you!" He shook the man gently.

"Mr. Grogan," he said, "wake up! Wake up!"

Homer ran to the water jar and filled a paper cup full of water. He ran back to the old operator, but he was afraid to follow the instructions he had been given. He put the cup down on the table and shook Mr. Grogan again.

"Mr. Grogan," he said. "Wake up! They're calling you!"

Homer splashed the cup of water into the telegraph operator's face. Mr. Grogan sat up with a start, opened his eyes, looked at Homer, listened to the telegraph box, and then answered the call.

"That's right," he said to the boy. "Now quick! A cup of black coffee. Hurry!"

Homer ran out of the office to Corbett's. When he got back, the old telegraph operator's eyes were almost closed again, but he was still doing his work.

"That's right, boy," he said. "Don't worry. Don't be afraid. That's exactly right."

Mr. Grogan stopped the telegrapher at the other end of the wire a moment and began to sip the coffee. "First splash the cold water," he said, "then fetch the black coffee."

"Yes, sir," Homer said. "Is it an important telegram?"

"No," Mr. Grogan said. "It is most *unimportant.* Business. The accumulating of money. It's a night letter. You won't have to deliver it tonight. Most unimportant. But very important for me to receive it."

He lifted his voice now because he was awake and strong again. "They've been wanting to retire me for years," he shouted. "They've been wanting to put in the machines they're inventing all over the place—Multiplexes and Teletypes," he said with contempt. "Machines instead of human beings!" He spoke softly now, as if to himself or to the people who were seeking to put him out of his place in the world. "I wouldn't know what to do with myself if I didn't have this job. I guess I'd die in a week. I've worked all my life and I'm not going to stop now."

"Yes, sir," Homer said.

"I know I can count on you to help me, boy," Mr. Grogan said, "because you have *already* helped me. Thank you, boy." He rattled the bug. The answer came, and he began to type the telegram, but as he typed he spoke with a kind of pride and vigor which pleased Homer very much. "Trying to put me out of my job!" he shouted. "Why, I was the fastest telegrapher in the world. Faster than Wolinsky, sending and receiving both—and no mistakes. Willie Grogan. Telegraph operators all over the world know that name. They know Willie Grogan was the best of them all!" He paused now and smiled at the messenger—the boy from the slums who had come to work last night, just in time.

"Sing another song, boy," he said, "for you and I are still alive."

Homer began to sing immediately.

CHAPTER 7

IF A MESSAGE COMES

Mrs. Macauley sat in the old rocking chair in the parlor of the house on Santa Clara Avenue waiting for her son to come home. He reached the parlor a little after midnight. He was grimy and tired and sleepy, but at the same time she could see that he was startled and restless. She knew that when he spoke his voice would be hushed, as the voice of her husband, this boy's father, had been. He stood a long time in the dark room, just being there. And then, instead of beginning with the things most important to talk about, he said, "Everything's all right, Ma. I don't want you to sit up this way *every* night."

He paused and had to say again, "Everything's all right."

"I know," his mother said. "Now sit down."

He moved to sit in the old overstuffed chair but instead he collapsed. His mother smiled.

"Well," she said, "I know you're tired, but I can see you're troubled, too. What is it?"

The boy waited a moment and then began to speak very swiftly, but very quietly too. "I had to deliver a telegram to a lady over on G Street," he said. "She was a Mexican lady." He stopped suddenly and got to his feet.

"I don't know how to tell you about this," he said, "because—well, the telegram was from the War Department. Her son was killed, but she wouldn't believe it. She just wouldn't believe it. I never saw anybody heartbroken that way before. She made me eat candy—made out of cactus. She hugged me and said *I* was her boy. I didn't care about that if it made her happy. I didn't even care about the candy." He stopped again. "She kept looking at me as if *I* were her boy and for a while I wasn't sure I wasn't, I felt so bad. When I got back to the office the old telegraph operator, Mr. Grogan—he was drunk, just as he said he would be. I did what he *told* me to—I splashed water in his face and got him a cup of black coffee to keep him awake. If he doesn't do his work they'll put him on a pension, and he doesn't want that. I got him sober all right and he did his work all right and then he told me about himself, and then we sang. I guess it was silly, but it makes me feel sad."

He stopped talking to walk about the room a moment. He went on, standing at the open door and looking away from his mother. "All of a sudden," he said, "I feel lonely--not like I ever felt before. Even when Papa died I didn't feel *this* way, because —well, we all looked to you and you didn't let us feel anything was changed. And nothing *was* changed. Everything was all right. I don't know what it is, but now everything *is* changed." And then he said with all the finality of youth, *"Everything—"*

He turned away from the open door to face his mother. "In two days," he said, "everything is different. I'm lonely and I don't know what I'm lonely *for.*" Now, moving closer, he said, "Ma?"

His mother didn't reply, waiting for him to go on. "I don't know what's happening in the world," he said, "or why it's happening, but no matter what happens, don't let anything hurt *you* that way. Everything *is* changed, but don't let it change too much for *us.*"

The woman smiled and waited to see if he had anything more to say, and as he didn't she began to speak. "Everything *is* changed," she said—"for you. But it is still the same, too. The loneliness you feel has come to you because you are no longer a child. But the whole world has always been full of that loneliness. The loneliness does not come from the War. The War did not make it. It was the loneliness that made the War. It was the despair in all things for no longer having in them the grace of God. We'll stay together. We'll not change too much." She thought a moment and then told him what her answer would be to the most unwelcome event of this change in the world. "If a message comes to me," she said, "as to the Mexican woman tonight, I shall believe the *words* of it, but nothing more. And I shall not need to weep, because I know there can be no killing of my son." She stopped and then went on, almost cheerfully. "What did you have for supper?"

"Pie," Homer said—"apple and cocoanut cream. The manager of the office paid for them. He's the greatest guy I ever met."

"I'll send Bess with a lunch for you tomorrow," Mrs. Macauley said.

"I don't want any lunch," Homer said. "We like to go out and buy something and sit down and eat together. You don't have to go to the trouble of making a lunch and then send Bess with it. It's more fun going out and getting something." He stopped. "This job is a wonderful thing for me," he said, "but it sure makes school seem silly."

"Of course," Mrs. Macauley said. "Schools are only to keep children off the streets, but sooner or later they've got to go out into the streets, whether they like it or not. It's natural for fathers and mothers to be afraid of the world for their children but there's nothing for them to be afraid of. The world is full of frightened little children. Being frightened, they frighten each other. Try to understand," she went on. "Try to love everyone you meet. I shall be in this parlor waiting for you every night. But you needn't come and talk to me unless you wish to do so. I shall understand. I know there shall be times when your heart shall be unable to give your tongue one word of speech to utter." She stopped now and looked at the boy. "You're tired, I know, so go along to sleep."

"O.K., Ma," the boy said, and went to his room.

CHAPTER 8

BE PRESENT AT OUR
TABLE, LORD

At seven in the morning the alarm clock clicked
—that's all—and Homer Macauley sat up. He ad-
justed the clock so that the alarm would not go off.
He then got out of bed and brought out his body-
building course from New York and began reading
the instructions for the day. His brother Ulysses
watched, as he always did, awakening with Homer
at the click just before the alarm, which Homer
never allowed to go off. The body-building course
from New York consisted of a printed booklet and
an elastic stretcher. Homer turned to Lesson 7 while

Ulysses crowded in under his arm to be nearer the fabulous stuff. After some ordinary preliminary exercises, including deep breathing, Homer lay flat on his back and lifted his legs stiffly from the floor.

"What's that?" Ulysses said.

"Exercises."

"What for?"

"Muscle."

"Going to be the strongest man in the world?" Ulysses said.

"Naaah," Homer said.

"What are you going to be, then?"

"You go back to sleep," Homer said.

Ulysses obediently got back in bed but sat up, watching. At last Homer began to get dressed.

"Where are you going?" the younger brother said.

"School," the older said.

"Going to learn something?"

"I'm going to run the two-twenty low hurdles."

"Where are you going to run them?"

"I'm not going to run them anywhere. They're wood frames every ten or fifteen yards that you've got to jump over as you run."

"Why?"

"Well," Homer said almost impatiently, "it's a foot race. Two-twenty low hurdles. Everybody born in this town runs the two-twenty low hurdles. It's the big race of Ithaca. The manager of the telegraph office where I work ran the two-twenty low hurdles when *he* went to Ithaca High. He was Valley Champion."

"What's Valley Champion?" Ulysses said.

"That's the best."

"You going to be the best?"

"Well," Homer said, "I'm going to try. Now go back to sleep."

Ulysses slipped down in bed, but as he did so he said, "Tomorrow—" then corrected himself— "*yesterday* I saw the train."

Homer knew what his brother was telling him. He smiled remembering his own fascination with the passing of the train. "How was it?" he said.

Ulysses remembered soberly. "There was a black man, waved," he said.

"Did you wave back to him?" Homer said.

"First I waved first," Ulysses said. "Then he waved first. Then I waved. Then he waved. He sang 'Kentucky, weep no more.' "

"Yeah?"

"He said, 'Going home!' " Ulysses said and looked at his brother. "When are *we* going home?"

"We're home now," Homer said.

"Then why didn't he come here?"

"Everybody's got a different home. Some East, some West, some North, some South. We're West."

"Is West the best?"

"I don't know," Homer said. "I haven't been anywhere else."

"Are you going?"

"Some day."

"Where?"

"New York."

"Where's New York?"

"East. After New York, London. After London, Paris. After Paris, Berlin. Then Vienna, Rome, Moscow, Stockholm—some day I'm going to all the great cities of the world."

"Going to come back?"

"Sure."

"Going to be glad?"

"Sure."

"Why?"

"Well," Homer said, "because— Going to be glad to see Ma and Marcus and Bess." And then he looked at his brother. "Going to be glad to see *you*. And Mary Arena next door, and her father Mr. Arena. Going to be glad to come home and sit down and talk and listen to some music and sing and have supper together."

The little brother pleaded earnestly. "Don't go,' he said. "Homer, don't go!"

"I'm not going *now*," the older brother said. "Now I'm going to school."

"Don't *ever* go," Ulysses said. "Papa went, and he didn't come back. Marcus went. Don't you go too, Homer."

"It's going to be a long time before I go," Homer said. "So you go to sleep."

Be Present at Our Table, Lord

"All right," Ulysses said. "Going to run the twenty-two?"

"The *two-twenty*," Homer said. "The two-twenty low hurdles."

When Homer sat down at the breakfast table his sister Bess and his mother were waiting for him. The family bowed their heads a moment, lifted them and began to eat.

"What prayer did you say?" Bess said to her brother.

"The prayer I *always* say," Homer said, and then quoted it, saying the words exactly as he had learned to say them when he had scarcely known how to speak.

> "Be present at our table, Lord.
> Be here and everywhere adored.
> These creatures bless, and grant that we
> May feast in Paradise with Thee.
> Amen."

"Oh, that's old," Bess said, "and besides, you don't even know what you're saying."

"I know all right," Homer said. "I may say it a little too swiftly because I'm hungry, but I know what it means. It's the spirit of the thing that counts anyway. What prayer did *you* say?"

"You've got to tell me first what the words mean," Bess said.

"What do *you* mean what do they mean?" Homer said. "They mean exactly what they say."

"Well," Bess said, "what *do* they say?"

"Be present at our table, Lord," Homer said. "Well, that means—Be present at our table, Lord. Lord means a lot of things, I guess, but I guess all the things it means are good. Be here and everywhere adored—well, that means let good things be loved here and everywhere else. These creatures—that means us, I guess—everybody. Bless—that means—well, bless. Bless means to forgive maybe, I guess. Or to love, maybe, or to watch over, or something like that. I don't know for sure but I guess it's something like that. And grant that we may feast in Paradise with Thee. Well, that means exactly what it says. Just grant that we may feast in Paradise with Thee."

"Who is *Thee?*" Bess said.

Homer turned to his mother. "Doesn't the prayer mean," he said, "that if people are right, they feast in Paradise every time they sit down at a table? Thee is good things, isn't it?"

"Of course," Mrs. Macauley said.

"But isn't Thee *somebody?*" Bess said.

"Sure," Homer said. "But I'm somebody too. Ma and you and everybody is somebody. Grant that this world is Paradise and that everybody we ever have food with is somebody. Bess," Homer said impatiently, "it's a table prayer, and you know as well as I do what it means. You just want to mix me up. Well, don't worry. You can. I guess *anybody* can mix me up, but it doesn't make any difference because I *believe*. Everybody believes. Don't they, Ma?"

"Of course they do," Mrs. Macauley said. "If you don't believe, you're not alive. And you can't feast at all, let alone in Paradise—no matter how laden with wonderful food your table is. It's faith that makes anything wonderful—not the thing itself."

"You see," Homer said to Bess, and then dismissed the discussion once and for all. "I'm going to run the two-twenty low hurdles at the track meet today," he said.

"Is that so?" Mrs. Macauley said. "Why?"

"Well, Ma, it's an important race," Homer said. "Mr. Spangler ran it when *he* went to Ithaca High. You've got to run and jump *both* in that race. He carries a hard-boiled egg around with him for luck."

"Carrying a hard-boiled egg around for luck," Bess said, "is superstition."

"Well, what's the difference?" Homer said. "Superstition or anything else. He sent me for two day-old pies from Chatterton's—apple and cocoanut cream. Two for a quarter. Fresh pies are a quarter each, so if you've got only a quarter to spend, you get only one. Day-old pies are *two* for a quarter, so you get two. Half of each pie for me and half for Mr. Grogan—but he can only eat one or two slices altogether. That gives me a lot of pie to eat. Mr. Grogan likes to drink more than eat."

Mary Arena, the neighbor girl, came into the

kitchen by way of the back door. She brought with her a small Woolworth bowl and put it on the table. Homer got up.

"Here, Mary," he said. "Sit down and have breakfast with us."

"I just had breakfast with Papa and sent him to work," Mary said. "Thanks just the same. I brought some stewed dried peaches that I made for Papa, Mrs. Macauley."

"Thank you, Mary," Mrs. Macauley said. "How is Papa?"

"Papa's just fine," Mary said. "Morning or night, though, he likes to tease me. First thing this morning when he came to the table he said, 'Any letters? Any letters from Marcus yet?' "

"We'll be getting another letter soon," Bess said. She got up from the table. "Come on, Mary," she said. "Let's go."

"All right, Bess," Mary said, and then turned to Mrs. Macauley. "But to tell you the truth, Mrs. Macauley," she said, "I'm getting sick and tired of going to college. It's just like high school. I'm too old to be going to school all the time. Times have changed. I honest-to-goodness would like to go out and find myself a job somewhere."

"And so would I," Bess said.

"Nonsense," Mrs. Macauley said. "You're both children— Seventeen years old. Your father has a good job, Mary, and your *brother*, Bess."

Be Present at Our Table, Lord

"But it just doesn't seem right, Mrs. Macauley," Mary said. "It doesn't seem right to just go to school when Marcus is in the Army and the whole world is gouging each other's eyes out. I sometimes wish I was a man, so I could be in the Army with Marcus. We could have a lot of fun together, I bet."

"Now don't you worry, Mary," Mrs. Macauley said. "This will all pass. Everything will be the same as ever before we know it."

"Well," Mary said, "I hope so," and then went along with her friend Bess Macauley to school.

Homer watched the girls go. After a moment he spoke. "What about *that*, Ma?" he said.

"Why, it's perfectly natural," Mrs. Macauley said, "for a couple of girls to want to get out and flap their wings."

"I don't mean wanting to get out and flap their wings," Homer said. "I mean Mary."

"Mary is a sweet, unaffected, childlike girl," Mrs. Macauley said. "She is the most childlike girl I've ever known, and I'm glad Marcus is in love with her. Marcus couldn't find a sweeter girl."

"Ma," Homer said impatiently, "I know all about *that*. That isn't what I'm talking about. Don't you see?" He paused, then added suddenly as if it were no use trying to talk about the feeling he had—the feeling that there would be pain out of the War for many people who would never get near it. "Oh, well, I'll see you tonight when I get home. So long."

Mrs. Macauley watched him go, wondering what

it was he had wanted to tell her. Suddenly out of the corner of her eye she saw somebody—very small. It was Ulysses in his nightshirt. He looked up at her, almost as a small animal looks up at that creature of its kind which is its greatest delight and comfort. The expression of his face was deeply serious and incredibly charming. Ulysses said, "Why does he say, 'Weep no more, Weep no more'?"

"Who?" Mrs. Macauley said.

"The black man on the train."

"It's a song, Ulysses," Mrs. Macauley said. She took his hand. "Come on, now, put on your clothes."

"Will the black man be on the train again today?" the little boy said.

Mrs. Macauley thought a moment. "Yes," she said.

CHAPTER 9

RABBITS AROUND HERE
SOMEWHERE

On his way to school Homer Macauley passed a
picket fence protecting an empty lot full of weeds
on San Benito Avenue. The fence was old and rotten
and had no use other than to ornament with majestic
ridicule a small area of waste, and to protect a bored
group of weed tribes which surely needed no protection. The daytime school student and nighttime
telegraph messenger brought his bicycle to a dy-
namic skidding halt, dropped the contraption and
hurried to the fence as if there he would discover
something extremely fleeting and apt to be lost if

he did not hurry. The fence was about a foot higher than the regulation low hurdles, and as for anything fleeting being there, whatever it might be, it was fleeting with a swiftness that would take a century. Homer studied the fence, the area beyond it, the running area before it, and then measured the height of the fence, which was considerably above his waist. He now rehearsed a few jumps, went back ten yards, and then without any announcement from himself to himself he turned in a fury and ran toward the fence. When he was near enough he made a beautiful hurdle, kicked the fence, knocked down part of it, and himself fell in the weeds, but got right up and went back for another try. The wood of the fence broke easily, making a sound that was nobly unnecessary and therefore comical. Altogether Homer made seven tries, not one of which was successful. He stopped only when the whole fence had been brought down into still greater ruin.

An old man with a walking stick came out of the house across the street, smoking a pipe, and quietly watched Homer. Just as Homer was getting up from the last spill and was brushing himself off, the man spoke.

"What are you doing?" he said.

"Hurdling," Homer said.

"Hurt yourself?"

"Naaah," Homer said. "The fence is a little too high, that's all. The weeds are slippery too."

Rabbits Around Here Somewhere

The old man looked at the weeds a moment and then said, "Those are milkweeds. They make very good feed for rabbits. Rabbits like them. I used to have a hutch of rabbits about eleven years ago, but somebody opened the door in the middle of the night and they all ran away."

"What did he open the door for?" Homer said.

"Well, I don't know," the old man said. "I never did find out who did it. I lost thirty-three head of the prettiest rabbits you ever saw. Pink-eyes, cat-faces, Belgians, and two or three other kinds—never did find out."

"You like rabbits?" Homer said.

"They're gentle little animals," the old man said. "Domestic rabbits are very mild-mannered." The man looked around among the weeds of the empty lot. "Thirty-three rabbits out in the open for eleven years," he said. "Well, there's no telling how many of them there are now—not the way *they* breed—or how *wild* they are, either. I wouldn't be surprised," he said, "if this whole city is full of wild rabbits now."

"*I* never see any of them," Homer said.

"Maybe not," the old man said. "But they're here —somewhere. The whole city's overrun with them, most likely. A couple more years and they'll be a serious problem."

Even so, Homer got on his bike. "Well," he said, "I got to go now. I'll be seeing you."

"You bet," the old man said. "My name's Charles

49

—just call me Charlie. Any time at all. You're welcome to it."

"Yes, sir," Homer said. Then he went back to his own theme. "Going to run the two-twenty low hurdles at the high school track meet this afternoon," he told the old man.

"Never did go to high school myself," the old man said, "but I fought in the Spanish-American War."

"Yes, sir," Homer said. "Well, so long!"

"Oh, yes," the old man said, but he was talking to himself. "Spanish-American War," he said. "Ran like a rabbit half the time."

Homer disappeared around the corner on his bicycle. The old man strolled back to his little broken-down house, puffing his pipe and looking around. He poked his walking stick into a big weed. "Rabbits around here somewhere," he said. "Wild by this time—not the way they used to be."

CHAPTER 10

ANCIENT HISTORY

On the track of the athletic field of Ithaca High School the hurdles were set for the 220-yard low hurdle race. Now, in the morning, four boys were running a practice race. Each ran well, under control, and each hurdled with good form. Coach Byfield, stop-watch in hand, came up to the winner.

"That was better, Ackley," he said to a boy who was surely not common, but for all that surely not terribly *uncommon* either. He was a boy who had the resigned manner of one whose family had not in recent decades been in want of food, clothing or shelter, who on occasion entertained others of similar good fortune.

"You've got a lot to learn yet," the coach said to the boy, "but I think you will be able to win the race this afternoon."

"I'll try my best, sir," the boy said.

"Yes, I know," the coach said. "You won't be having any competition today, but you will have plenty of it two weeks from now in the Valley Meet. Go to the shower now and take it easy until this afternoon."

"Yes, sir," the boy replied. He moved away, then stopped suddenly. "Excuse me, sir," he said. "How is my time?"

"Not bad," the coach said, "but not too good either. I wouldn't worry about the time, though. Just run the race I've taught you to run, and I think you'll come in first."

The other three runners were over to one side, watching and listening.

"He may *act* like a sissy," one of the boys said to the others, "but he always comes in first. What's the matter with you, Sam?"

"What's the matter with *me?*" Sam said. "What's the matter with *you?* Why don't *you* beat him?"

"I came in second."

"Second's no better than third," the other boy said.

"Hubert Ackley the Third, beating us!" Sam said. "We ought to be ashamed of ourselves."

"Sure," the second boy said, "but we've got no alibis. He just runs a better race, that's all."

The coach turned to these three and in an altogether different tone of voice, he said, "O.K., you guys—keep moving. You're not so good you can stand around and be proud of yourselves. Get to your marks and give it another try."

Without a word the boys went to their marks and the coach sent them off for another run of the race. After they began to run, the coach decided he would run them a couple more times before the afternoon meet. He seemed to want Hubert Ackley III to win the race.

The ancient history classroom was swiftly filling as the teacher, old Miss Hicks, waited for the final bell and the kind of order and quiet which in her class was the sign for the beginning of another stab at the problem of trying to educate, if not entertain, the boys and girls of Ithaca, now at high school and soon, at least theoretically, to be ready for the world. Homer Macauley, troubled by something that bordered on a state of adoration, studied a girl named Helen Eliot who walked from the door to her desk. Without a doubt this girl was the most beautiful girl in the world. Besides that, she was a snob—which Homer refused to believe was natural or permanent. Even so, and even though he worshiped her, the bitterest enemy of his school life was this snobbery of Helen Eliot. Following her came Hubert Ackley III. When Hubert reached Helen the two whispered a moment, irritating Homer very much. The final bell rang, and the teacher said, "All right. Silence, please. Who's absent?"

"I am," a boy said. His name was Joe Terranova, and he was the low comedian of the class. The four or five of Joe's faithful, the members of his comic religious cult, his worshipers, were instant in their response and appreciation of his swift and goofy wit. But Helen Eliot and Hubert Ackley turned and frowned at these Holy Rollers of the classroom, these bad-mannered offspring of slum-dwellers. This in turn angered Homer so much that when everyone else had ceased laughing he burst out with an artificial "Ha-ha-ha," which he sent almost directly into the faces of Hubert, whom he despised, and Helen, whom he adored. Then he turned swiftly to Joe and said, "As for you, Joe, shut up when Miss Hicks is talking."

"Now, none of your nonsense, Joseph," Miss Hicks said. And turning to Homer, "Or yours, young man." She paused a moment to look the class over. "Now," she said, "we will take up the Assyrians where we left off yesterday. I want everyone's undivided attention—everyone's *continuous* undivided attention. First we will read from our ancient history textbook. Then we will have an oral discussion of what we have read."

The low comedian could not resist this opportunity for horseplay. "No, Miss Hicks," he suggested. "Let's not discuss it orally. Let's discuss it silently, so I can sleep." Again the faithful roared with laughter and the snobs turned away, disgusted. Miss Hicks did not answer the comedian immediately, for on the one hand it was difficult not to enjoy the swiftness of his wit and on the other hand it was equally difficult to know how to cope with him so that the wit would continue. And yet it was absolutely necessary to keep him in line. At last she spoke.

"You must not be unkind, Joseph," she said, "especially when it happens that you are right and —I am wrong."

"Well, I'm sorry, Miss Hicks," the comedian said. "I guess I just can't help it. Oral discussion! What other kind of discussion is there? But O.K., I'm sorry." Now, with a kind of spoofing of himself and of his own presumptuousness, he waved to her, saying patronizingly, "Go ahead, Miss Hicks."

"Thank you," the teacher said. "Now, everybody —wide awake!"

"Wide awake!" Joe said. "Look at them—they're all half asleep."

Even though the old teacher was enjoying Joe's sallies, it was necessary for her to say, "Another interruption, Joseph, and I will have to ask you to go to the principal's office."

"I'm only trying to get myself a little education," the comedian said. "But just look at them. They're half asleep, aren't they?" And then he surveyed the faces of the pupils of the classroom and added, "All my pals, too. Great baseball players."

"Ah, shut up, Joe," Homer said to his friend. "You don't have to show off all the time. Everybody knows how smart you are."

"Not another word," Miss Hicks said. "Not another word from either *one* of you. Now," she said, "turn to page 117, paragraph two." Everyone turned to this page and found the place. "Ancient history," the teacher continued, "may *seem* to be a dull and unnecessary study. At a time like the present, when so much history is going on in our own world, another world—long since ended—may seem useless to study and understand. Such a notion, however, is incorrect. It is very important for us to know of other times, other cultures, other peoples, and other worlds. Who'll volunteer to come to the head of the class and read?" Two girls and Hubert Ackley III raised their hands.

Joe, the comedian, turned to Homer, and said, "Look at that guy, will you?"

Of the two girls who had volunteered the teacher selected Helen Eliot, the beautiful and snobbish. Homer, fascinated, watched her walk to the front of the class. She just stood there, being very beautiful for a moment, and then in the purest and most attractive voice imaginable she began to read, while Homer marveled at the incredible miracle of such a body and such a voice.

"The Assyrians," Helen Eliot read, "long of nose, hair and beard, developed Nineveh in the north to a position of great power. After many vicissitudes with the Hittites, Egyptians and others, they conquered Babylon under the reign of Tiglath Pileser the First, in eleven hundred B.C. For centuries afterward, the power veered between Nineveh built of stone and Babylon built of brick. There is no connection between the names 'Syrian' and 'Assyrian,' and the Assyrians were to fight the Syrians until Tiglath Pileser the Third conquered them and exiled the ten lost tribes of Israel."

Helen paused for a fresh supply of breath with which to read the next paragraph, but before she could begin to read again, Homer Macauley said, "How about Hubert *Ackley* the Third? Who did *he* conquer, or what did he do?"

The well-bred boy got to his feet in a kind of decent bitterness. "Miss Hicks," he said very earnestly, "I cannot allow such willful mischievousness to go uncorrected or unpunished. I must ask you to order Mr. Macauley to go to the principal's office— or," he said very deliberately, "I shall have to take the matter into my own hands."

Homer jumped out of his seat. "Ah, shut up," he said. "Your name *is* Hubert Ackley the Third isn't it? Well, what did you ever do, or for that matter what did Hubert Ackley the Second ever do, or what did Hubert Ackley the First ever do?" He paused a moment and turned to Miss Hicks and then to Helen Eliot. "I think that's a good intelligent question," he said. Then he turned to Hubert Ackley and repeated the question. "What did they do?"

"Well," Hubert said, "at least no Ackley has ever been a common—" He stopped to seek an appropriately withering word, and then said, "—fanfaron," a word nobody else in Ithaca had ever heard before.

"Fanfaron?" Homer said. He turned to the teacher. "What's that mean, Miss Hicks?" he said. As she was not ready with a definition of the word, Homer turned quickly to Hubert Ackley and went on, "Listen, number three," he said, "don't be calling me names I never even *heard* before."

"A fanfaron," Hubert said, "is a hoodlum—a braggart." And he stopped to find another, *lower* word.

"Ah, shut up," Homer said.

He turned to Helen Eliot and smiled the famous Macauley smile. *"Fanfaron!"* he repeated. "What kind of cussing is that?" Then he sat down.

Helen Eliot waited for a sign from the teacher to go on reading. Miss Hicks, however, did not give the sign. Finally Homer understood. He got to his feet and said to Hubert Ackley III, "All right, I apologize. I'm sorry."

"Thank you," the well-bred boy said, and sat down.

The ancient-history teacher looked about the room a moment and then said, "Homer Macauley

and Hubert Ackley will remain in their seats after
school."

"But, Miss Hicks," Homer said, "what about the
school track meet?"

"I'm not interested in the school track meet," the
teacher said. "The development of your manners is
as important as the development of your bodies. Perhaps more important."

"Miss Hicks," Hubert Ackley said, "Ithaca High
School is counting on me to win the two-twenty low
hurdle race this afternoon and two weeks from now
to make a good showing in the Valley Track Meet.
I'm afraid Coach Byfield will *insist* on my taking
part."

"I don't know about Coach Byfield *insisting*,"
Homer said, "but *I'm* going to run the two-twenty
low hurdles this afternoon—that's all."

Hubert Ackley looked at Homer. "I had no idea,"
he said, "you had gone out for that race."

"Well," Homer said, "I have." He turned to the
teacher. "Miss Hicks, if you let us go this time, I
promise never again to make any trouble or to be
disobedient or *anything*. And so does Hubert." He
turned to Hubert and said, "Don't you?"

"Yes, I do, Miss Hicks," Hubert said.

"You will both stay in after school," the ancient-
history teacher said. "Helen, please continue to
read."

"The allied armies," Helen read, "of the Chal-
deans from the south and the Medes and Persians

from the north overcame the Assyrian empire and Nineveh bowed to their might. Nebuchadnezzar the Second ruled over the second Babylonian empire. Then came the great Cyrus, King of Persia, with his hordes of invaders. His conquest, however, was only one of a cycle, for the descendants of this army would later be subjugated by Alexander the Great."

Homer, disgusted now, tired from the work of the night before and lulled by the sweet voice of the girl he believed was made only for himself, slowly dropped his head on his folded arms and began to enjoy something almost the equivalent of sleep. Still he could hear the girl reading.

"From this melting pot," she read, "the world has a heritage of great value. The Mosaic code of the Bible owes some of its principles to some of the laws formulated by Hammurabi, who was called the lawgiver. From their system of arithmetic, in which they used the multiple of twelve as well as our familiar ten, we derive our sixty minutes to the hour and 360 degrees to the circle. Arabia gave us our numerals, which are still called Arabic to distinguish them from the Roman system of notation. The Assyrians invented the sundial. The modern apothecary symbols and the signs of the Zodiac originated with the Babylonians. Comparatively recent excavations in Asia Minor have revealed that there was a magnificent empire there."

"A magnificent empire?" Homer dreamed. "Where? Ithaca? Ithaca in California? Away out to hell and gone? Without any great people, without any great discoveries, without sundials, without numerals, without Zodiacs, without humor, without anything? Where was this great empire?" He decided to sit up again and look around. He saw only the face of Helen Eliot, perhaps the greatest empire of them all, and he heard her wondrous voice, perhaps the greatest achievement of pathetic mankind.

"The Hittites," she said, "had swung down the coast and over into Egypt. They mingled their blood with the Hebrew tribes and gave to the Hebrews the Hittite nose."

Helen stopped reading and turned to the ancient-history teacher. "That's the end of the chapter, Miss Hicks," she said.

"Very well, Helen," Miss Hicks said. "Thank you for an excellent reading. You may be seated."

CHAPTER 11

A SPEECH ON THE HUMAN NOSE

Miss Hicks waited for Helen to take her seat and then looked over the faces of her pupils. "Now," she said, "what have we learned?"

"That people all over the world have noses," Homer said.

Miss Hicks was not upset by this reply and took it for what it was worth. "What else?" she said.

"That noses," Homer said, "are not only for blowing or to have colds in but also to keep the record of ancient history straight."

Miss Hicks turned away from Homer and said,

A Speech on the Human Nose

"Someone else, please. Homer seems to have been carried away by the noses."

"Well, it's in the book, isn't it?" Homer said. "What do *they* mention it for? It must be important."

"Perhaps," Miss Hicks said, "you would like to make an extemporaneous speech on the nose, Mr. Macauley."

"Well," Homer said, "maybe not exactly a speech —but ancient history tells us one thing." Slowly now, and with a kind of unnecessary emphasis, he continued, "People have always had noses. To prove it all you have to do is look around at everybody in this classroom." He looked around at everybody. "Noses," he said, "all over the place." He stopped a moment to decide what else would be possible to say on this theme. "The nose," he decided to say, "is perhaps the most ridiculous part of the human face. It has always been a source of embarrassment to the human race, and the Hittites probably beat up on everybody because their noses were so big and crooked. It doesn't matter who invented the sundial because sooner or later somebody invents a watch. The important thing is, Who's got the noses?"

Joe the comedian listened with profound interest and admiration, if not envy. Homer continued.

"Some people," he said, "talk through their noses. A great many people snore through their noses, and a handful of people whistle or sing through them. Some people are led around by their noses, others

63

use the nose for prying and poking into miscellaneous places. Noses have been bitten by mad dogs and movie actors in passionate love stories. Doors have been slammed on them and they have been caught in egg-beaters and automatic record changers. The nose is stationary, like a tree, but being on a movable object—the head—it suffers great punishment by being taken to places where it is only in the way. The purpose of the nose is to smell what's in the air, but some people sniff with the nose at other people's ideas, manners, or appearances." He turned and looked at Hubert Ackley III and then at Helen Eliot, whose nose, instead of moving upward, for some reason went slightly downward. "These people," he said, "generally hold their noses toward heaven, as if that were the way to get in. Most animals have nostrils but few have noses, as we understand noses, yet the sense of smell in animals is more highly developed than in man—who has a nose, and no fooling." Homer Macauley took a deep breath and decided to conclude his speech. "The most important thing about the nose," he said, "is that it makes trouble, causes wars, breaks up old friendships, and wrecks many happy homes. *Now* can I go to the track meet, Miss Hicks?"

The ancient-history teacher, although pleased with this imaginative discourse on a trivial theme, would not allow its success to interfere with the need for her to maintain order in her classroom. "You will stay in after school, Mr. Macauley," she said.

"and *you*, Mr. Ackley. Now that we have disposed of the matter of noses, someone else please comment on what we have read."

There were no comments.

"Come, come now," Miss Hicks said. "Somebody else comment—*anybody*."

Joe the comedian answered the call. "Noses are red," he said, "violets are blue. This class is dead. And in all probability so are you."

"Anyone else?" Miss Hicks said.

"Big noses are generally on navigators and explorers," a girl said.

"All two-headed boys have two noses," Joe said.

"The nose is never on the back of the head," one of Joe's admirers said.

"Somebody else," Miss Hicks said. She turned to a boy and said his name. "Henry?"

"I don't know anything about noses," Henry said.

Joe turned to Henry. "All right," he said, "who is Moses?"

"Moses was in the Bible," Henry said.

"Did he have a nose?" Joe said.

"Sure he had a nose," Henry said.

"All right, then," Joe said. "Why don't you say, 'Moses had a nose as big as most noses'? This is an ancient history class. Why don't you try to learn something once in a while? Moses—noses—ancient—history. Catch on?"

Henry tried to catch on. "Moses noses," he said. "No, wait a minute. Moses's nose was a big nose."

"Ah," Joe said. "You'll never learn anything. You'll die in the poorhouse. Moses had a nose as big as most noses! Henry, you've got to get that straight. Now think about it."

"All right, now," Miss Hicks said, "anybody else?"

"The hand is faster than the eye," Joe said, "but only the nose runs."

"Miss Hicks," Homer said, "you've got to let me run the two-twenty low hurdles."

"I'm not interested in *any* kind of hurdles," Miss Hicks said. "Now, anyone else?"

"Well," Homer said, "I brought this class to life for you, didn't I? I've got them all talking about noses, haven't I?"

"That's beside the point," the ancient-history teacher said. "Somebody else now?"

But it was too late. The class bell rang. Everyone got up to leave for the track meet except Homer Macauley and Hubert Ackley III.

CHAPTER 12

THE TWO-TWENTY LOW
HURDLE RACE

The boys' athletic coach of Ithaca High School stood in the office of the principal of Ithaca High School—a man whose last name was Ek, a circumstance duly reported by Mr. Robert Ripley in a daily newspaper cartoon entitled "Believe It or Not." Mr. Ek's first name was Oscar, and not worthy of notice.

"Miss Hicks," the principal of Ithaca High School said to the coach of Ithaca High School, "is the oldest and by far the best teacher we have ever had at this school. She was *my* teacher when I attended Ithaca High School and she was your teacher, too,

Mr. Byfield. I'm afraid I wouldn't care to go over her head about punishing a couple of unruly boys."

"Hubert Ackley the Third is *not* an unruly boy," the coach said. "Homer Macauley—yes. Hubert Ackley—no. He is a perfect little gentleman."

"Yes," the principal said, "Hubert Ackley *does* come from a well-to-do family. But if Miss Hicks has asked him to stay in after school, then *in* it is. He *is* a perfect little gentleman, no doubt. His *father* was, I remember. Perfect—perfect. But Miss Hicks is the teacher of the ancient history class and she has never been known to punish anyone who has not deserved to be punished. Hubert Ackley will have to be satisfied to run the race some other time."

The matter was surely closed now, the principal felt. The coach turned and left the office. He did not go to the athletic field, however. He went to the ancient history classroom instead. There he found Homer and Hubert and Miss Hicks. He bowed to the old teacher and smiled.

"Miss Hicks," he said, "I have spoken to Mr. Ek about this matter." The implication of his remark was that he had been given authorization to come and liberate Hubert Ackley III. Homer Macauley, however, leaped to his feet as if it were *he* who was to be liberated.

"Not *you*," the coach said with a tone of contempt. He turned to the other boy and said, "Mr. Ackley."

"What do you mean?" the ancient-history teacher ~aid.

The Two-Twenty Low Hurdle Race

"Mr. Ackley," the coach said, "is to get into his track suit immediately and run the two-twenty low hurdles. We're waiting for him."

"Oh yeah?" Homer said. He was overflowing with righteous indignation. "Well," he said, "what about *me—Mr. Macauley?*" There was no reply from the coach, who walked out of the room followed by a somewhat troubled and confused young man—Hubert Ackley III.

"Did you see that, Miss Hicks?" Homer Macauley shouted. "Is that special privilege or not?"

The ancient-history teacher was so upset by what had happened that she could barely speak.

"Mr. Byfield," she whispered softly, "is fitted to teach athletics only to jackasses like himself." She paused to observe the unworthiness of her remark. "I'm sorry," she said. "But the man is not only ignorant, he is a liar!" It was delightful to see Miss Hicks with so much natural and uncontrollable bitterness. It made Homer feel that she was just about the best teacher ever.

"I never did like him," Homer said. "It sure is good to know that you don't like him either."

"I have taught ancient history at Ithaca High School thirty-five years," Miss Hicks said. "I have been the school mother of hundreds of Ithaca boys and girls. I taught your brother Marcus and your sister Bess, and if you have younger brothers or sisters at home I shall some day teach them too."

"Just a brother, Miss Hicks," Homer said. "His name is Ulysses. How was Marcus in school?"

"Marcus and Bess," Miss Hicks said, "were both good—honest and civilized. Yes," she said, *"civilized,"* and she emphasized the word very carefully. "The behavior of ancient peoples had made them civilized from birth. Like yourself, Marcus sometimes spoke out of turn, but he was never a liar. Now these inferior human beings, these Byfields of the world who were never anything but fools—they think of me as an old woman. He came here and deliberately lied to me—just as he had lied to me time and again when he sat in this classroom as a boy. He has learned nothing except to toady shamelessly to those he feels are superior."

"Yeah?" Homer said, urging the ancient-history teacher to go on with her criticism.

"I have seen better men pushed around by his kind," she said. "The kind who go through life lying and cheating and crowding out men who are above such behavior. The two-twenty low hurdles! *Low* indeed!" The ancient-history teacher was terribly hurt. She blew her nose and wiped her eyes.

"Ah, don't feel bad, Miss Hicks," Homer said. "I'll stay in. You can punish me for talking out of turn. I guess I've got it coming, but from now on I'm going to try to be good. I never did know that teachers are human beings like anybody else—and *better,* too! It's all right, Miss Hicks. You can punish me."

The Two-Twenty Low Hurdle Race

"I didn't keep you in to punish you, Homer Macauley," the ancient-history teacher said. "I have always kept in only those who have meant the most to me—I have kept them in to be nearer them. I still do not believe I am mistaken about Hubert Ackley. It was Mr. Byfield who made him disobey me. I was going to send both of you to the field after a moment, anyway. You were not kept in for punishment, but for education. I watch the growth of spirit in the children who come to my class, and I am made happy by every fresh evidence of that growth. You apologized to Hubert Ackley, and even though it embarrassed him to do so, because your apology made him unworthy, he graciously accepted your apology. I kept you in after school because I wanted to talk to both of you—one of you from a good well-to-do family, the other from a good poor family. Getting along in this world will be even more difficult for him than for you. I wanted you to know one another a little better. It is very important. I wanted to talk to *both* of you."

"I guess I like Hubert," Homer said, "only he seems to think he is better than the other boys."

"Yes, I know," the ancient-history teacher said. "I know how you feel, but every man in the world *is* better than someone else, and not as good as someone *else*. Joe Terranova is brighter than Hubert, but Hubert is just as honest in his own way. In a democratic state every man is the equal of every other man up to the point of exertion, and after that every man is free to exert himself to do good or not, to grow nobly or foolishly, as he wishes. I am eager for my boys and girls to exert themselves to do good and to grow nobly. What my children *appear* to be on the surface is no matter to me. I am fooled neither by gracious manners nor by bad manners. I am interested in what is truly beneath each kind of manners. Whether one of my children is rich or poor, Catholic or Protestant or Jew, white or black or yellow, brilliant or slow, genius or simple-minded, is no matter to me, if there is humanity in him—if he has a heart—if he loves truth and honor—if he respects his inferiors and loves his superiors. If the children of my classroom are human, I do not want them to be alike in their *manner* of being human. If they are not corrupt, it does not matter to me how they differ from one another. I want each of my children to be himself. I don't want you, Homer, to be like somebody else just to please me or to make my work easier. I would soon be weary of a classroom full of perfect little ladies and gentle-men. I want my children to be *people*—each one separate—each one special—each one a pleasant and exciting variation of all the others. I wanted Hubert Ackley here to listen to this with you—to understand with you that if at the present you do not like him and he does not like you, that is perfectly natural. I wanted him to know that each of you will begin to be truly human when, in spite of your natural dislike of one another, you still respect one another. That is what it means to be civilized—that is what we are to learn from a study of ancient history." The teacher stopped now a moment and looked at the boy who, for some reason that even he could not understand, was on the verge of tears.

"I'm glad I've spoken to you," she said, "rather than to anyone else I know. When you leave this school—long after you have forgotten *me*—I shall be watching for you in the world, and I shall never be startled by the good things I know you shall do." The ancient-history teacher blew her nose again and touched her handkerchief to her eyes. "Run along to the athletic field," she said. "Race against Hubert Ackley in the two-twenty low hurdles. If there isn't time to change to your track clothes, run as you are, even if everybody laughs at you. Before you go very far along in the world, you will hear laughter many times, and not the laughter of men alone, but the mocking laughter of things themselves seeking to embarrass and hold you back—but I know you will pay no attention to that laughter." The teacher sighed and said wearily, "Run along to the field, Homer Macauley. I shall be watching." The second son of the Macauley family of Santa Clara Avenue in Ithaca, California, turned and walked out of the room.

On the athletic field Hubert Ackley and the three boys who had already raced with him that day were taking their places in the lanes for the two-twenty low hurdle race. Homer reached the fifth lane just as the man with the pistol lifted his arm to start the race. Homer went to his mark with the others. He felt very good, but also very angry, and he believed that nothing in the world would be able to keep him from winning this race—the wrong kind of shoes, the wrong kind of clothes for running, no practice, or anything else. He would just naturally win the race.

Hubert Ackley, in the lane next to Homer's lane, turned to him and said, *"You* can't run this race— like *that."*

"No?" Homer said. "Wait and see."

Mr. Byfield, sitting in the grandstand, turned to the man next to him and said, "Who's that starting in the outside lane without track clothes?" Then he remembered who it was.

He decided to stop the race so that he could remove the fifth runner, but it was too late. The gun had been fired and the runners were running. Homer and Hubert took the first hurdle a little ahead of the others, each of them clearing nicely. Homer moved a little forward ahead of Hubert on the second hurdle and kept moving forward on the third, fourth, fifth, sixth, seventh and eighth hurdles. But close behind him was Hubert Ackley. The two boys exchanged words as they ran. On the first hurdle Hubert shouted, "Where did you learn to run like that?"

"Nowhere," Homer said. "I'm learning *now.*"

On the second hurdle, Hubert said, "What's the hurry? You're going too fast."

"I'm going to win the race," Homer said.

On the third hurdle Ackley said, "Who said so?"

And on the fourth hurdle Homer said, *"I* said so."

On the fifth hurdle Hubert said, "Slow down. This is a long race. You'll get tired." And then suddenly he shouted, "Oh—oh, look out! Here comes Byfield!"

Homer reached the ninth hurdle exactly when the coach of Ithaca High School reached it, coming in the opposite direction. Nevertheless, Homer hurdled. He hurdled straight into the open arms of the athletic coach and the man and the boy fell to the ground. Hubert Ackley stopped running and turned to the other runners. "Stay where you are," he shouted. "Let him get up. He's running a good race, and he's had interference." Homer got to his feet quickly and went on running. The instant he started, the others started running also.

Everyone in the grandstand, even Helen Eliot, was amazed at what was happening in the race. Now the ancient-history teacher, Miss Hicks, was at the finish line of the race. She was cheering, but she was cheering for *each* of the boys.

"Come on, Homer!" she said. "Come on, Hubert! Hurry, Sam!—George!—Henry!"

At the next to the last hurdle Hubert Ackley

caught up with Homer Macauley. "Sorry," he said, "I've got to do it."

"Go ahead," Homer said, "if you can."

Hubert Ackley ran a little in front of Homer and there was no longer far to go. Homer didn't clear the last hurdle, but he almost caught up with the front runner. The finish of the race was so close no one could tell whether Hubert Ackley won or whether Homer Macauley won. Sam, George and Henry came in soon after, and Miss Hicks, the ancient-history teacher, brought them all together.

"You ran beautifully," she said, "every one of you!"

"I'm sorry," Hubert Ackley said, "Miss Hicks. I should have stayed in, with Homer."

"It's all right now," Miss Hicks said, "and it was good of you to wait for Homer to get up when he was interfered with."

Furious and bitter and a little shocked by the fall he had taken, the coach of Ithaca High School came running toward the group which Miss Hicks had gathered around her.

"Macauley!" he shouted from a distance of fifteen yards. "For the remainder of this semester," he said, "for what you have just done, you are deprived of the privilege of taking part in any school sport activities."

The coach reached the group and stood glaring at Homer Macauley. The ancient-history teacher turned to him.

"Mr. Byfield," she said, "why are you punishing Homer Macauley?"

"Excuse me, Miss Hicks," the coach said. "I will make my decisions without any assistance from the ancient history department." He turned to Homer and said, "Do you understand?"

"Yes, sir," Homer said.

"Now go to my office and stay there until I tell you to go," Byfield said.

"Your office?" Homer said. "But I've got to go—" He suddenly remembered that he had to be at work at four o'clock. "What time is it?" he said.

Hubert Ackley looked at his wrist watch. "It's a quarter to four," he said.

"Go to my office!" Byfield shouted.

"But you don't understand, Mr. Byfield," Homer said. "I've got some place to go. I'll be late."

Joe Terranova came into the group. "Why should he stay after school?" Joe said. "He didn't do anything wrong."

The coach had already suffered too much. "You keep your dirty little wop mouth shut!" he shouted at Joe. Then he pushed the boy, who went sprawling. But before he had touched the ground, Joe Terranova shouted: "W-O-P?"

Homer tackled Mr. Byfield as if they were on a football field, at the same time saying, "You can't call a friend of mine names."

By the time Homer and Byfield were on the ground again, Joe Terranova was on his feet. In

77

a fury he leaped on Byfield so that the man was sprawled all over the place. The principal of the school, Mr. Ek, came running, breathless and bewildered.

"Gentlemen!" he said. "Boys, boys!" He dragged Joe Terranova off the athletic coach, who did not get to his feet.

"Mr. Byfield," the principal of the school said, "what is the meaning of this unusual behavior?"

Speechless, Byfield pointed to Miss Hicks.

Miss Hicks stood above the man. "I've told you many times, Mr. Byfield, not to push people around," she said. "They don't like it." She turned to the principal of the school. "Mr. Byfield," she said, "owes Joe Terranova an apology."

"Is that so? Is that so, Mr. Byfield?" Mr. Ek said.

"Joe's people are from Italy," Miss Hicks said. "They are not, however, to be referred to as wops."

Joe Terranova said, "He doesn't need to apologize to me. If he calls me names, I'll bust him in the mouth. If he beats me up, I'll get my brothers."

"Joseph!" Miss Hicks said. "You must allow Mr. Byfield to apologize. He is not apologizing to you or to your people. He is apologizing to our own country. You must give him the privilege of once again trying to be an American."

"Yes, that's so," the principal of the school said. "This is America, and the only foreigners here are those who forget that this *is* America." He turned to the man who was still sprawled on the ground. "Mr. Byfield," he commanded.

The athletic coach of Ithaca High School got to his feet. To no one in particular he said, "I apologize," and hurried away.

Joe Terranova and Homer Macauley went off together. Joe walked well, but Homer limped. He had hurt his left leg when Byfield had tried to stop him.

Miss Hicks and Mr. Ek turned to the thirty or forty boys and girls gathered around. They were of many types and many nationalities.

"All right, now," Miss Hicks said. "Go along home to your families," and as the children were all a little bewildered, she added, "Brighten up, brighten up—don't be so upset. This is nothing."

"Yes," the principal of the school said, "brighten up. The War isn't going to last forever."

The children broke up into groups and walked away.

CHAPTER 13

THE TRAP, MY GOD, THE TRAP!

When Homer Macauley swung onto his bicycle after the track meet to get to work as soon as possible, a man named Big Chris walked into Covington's Sporting Goods Store on Tulare Street. He was a huge man, tall, lean and hard, with a great blond beard. He had just come down from the hills around Piedra to see about some new grub and shells and traps. Mr. Covington, the founder and proprietor of the store, began immediately to demonstrate to Big Chris the workings of a rather involved new trap that had just been invented by a man out in Friant.

The Trap, My God, the Trap!

The trap was enormous and complicated. It was made of steel, lemonwood, springs and ropes. Its principle seemed to be to take the animal, swing it up and around, and hold it off its feet until the trapper arrived.

"This is brand new," Mr. Covington said, "invented by a man named Safferty out in Friant. He's applied for a patent and so far he's made only two of them, one a model, which he sent to the patent office, and this one, which he sent to me, to sell. The trap is for any kind of animal that walks. Mr. Safferty calls it 'The LIFT-THEM-OFF-THEIR-FEET, SWING-THEM-AROUND, AND-HOLD-THEM SAFFERTY ALL-ANIMAL TRAP.' He's asking twenty dollars for it. Of course the trap hasn't been tested, but as you can see for yourself, it is strong and could very likely lift, swing and hold a full grown bear with no difficulty at all."

Big Chris listened to the proprietor of the sporting goods store as a child listens, and behind him Ulysses Macauley listened with the same fascination, ducking in between the two men for a better view of the trap. Mr. Covington was under the impression that Ulysses belonged to Big Chris and Big Chris was under the impression that Ulysses belonged to Mr. Covington so that between the two of them they had no reason to account for the small boy's presence. As for Ulysses himself, he was under the impression that he belonged wherever there was something interesting to see.

"The remarkable thing about this trap," Mr. Covington said, "is that it will not *hurt* the animal, leaving the fur whole and undamaged. The trap is guaranteed by Mr. Safferty himself for a period of eleven years. This includes all parts—the pliancy of the wood, which is lemonwood, the endurance of the springs, the steel, the ropes, and all other parts. Mr. Safferty, although not a trapper himself, believes this is the most effective and humane trap in the world. A man close to seventy, he lives quietly in Friant, reading books and inventing things. He has invented, all told, thirty-seven separate and distinct items of practical usefulness." Mr. Covington stopped his work with the trap. "Now," he said, "I believe the trap is set."

Ulysses, crowding in to watch, moved too far: the trap closed on him gently but swiftly, lifted him off his feet, turned him around and held him three feet off the floor, straight out, horizontally, clamped in. No sound came from the boy, even though he was a little bewildered. Big Chris, however, did not take the event so lightly.

"Careful there!" he shouted to Covington. "I don't want your son to be hurt."

"My son?" Covington said. "I thought he was *your* son. I never saw the boy before in my life. He came in with you."

"He did?" Big Chris said. "I didn't notice. Well, now, hurry! Get him out of the trap—get him out!"

"Yes, sir," Covington said. "Now let me see."

The Trap, My God, the Trap

Big Chris was worried and confused. "What's your name, boy?" he said.

"Ulysses," the boy in the trap said.

"My name is Big Chris," the man from the hills said. "Now you just hold tight there, Ulysses, and the man here will get you right out and set you down on your feet." Big Chris turned to Mr. Covington. "Well, come on now," he said, "get the boy out. Get him out!"

Mr. Covington, however, was just as confused as Big Chris. "I'm not sure I remember how Mr. Safferty explained *that* part of the trap," he said. "Mr. Safferty didn't *demonstrate* the trap, you see, because—well—we didn't have anything to demonstrate it on. Mr. Safferty only *explained* it. I believe *this* is supposed to move out—no, it seems to be immovable."

Now Big Chris and Mr. Covington went to work on the trap together, Big Chris holding Ulysses so that if the trap opened suddenly Ulysses wouldn't fall on his face, and the other man fooling around with the various parts of the trap to see if anything would give way.

"Well, hurry now," Big Chris said. "Let's not keep the boy in the air all day. You're not hurt, are you, Ulysses?"

"No, sir," Ulysses said.

"Well, you just hold tight," Big Chris said. "We'll get you out of this." He looked at the boy and then said, "What made you crowd in there?"

"Watching," Ulysses said.

"Yes, it *is* a fascinating sort of contraption, isn't it?" Big Chris said. "Now the man here will get you right out and I won't let you fall. How old are you?"

"Four," Ulysses said.

"Four," Big Chris said. "Well, I'm fifty years older than you. Now the man here will get you right out, won't you?" And Big Chris turned to Mr. Covington. "What's *your* name?" he said.

"Walter Covington," Mr. Covington said. "I own this store."

"Well, that's fine," Big Chris said. "Now, Walter, get the boy out of the trap. Move that piece of wood there. I'm holding him. Don't you worry, Ulysses. What's your *father's* name?"

"Matthew," Ulysses said.

"Well, he's a lucky man to have a boy like you around," Big Chris said. "A fellow with his eyes open. I'd give the world to have a boy like you, Ulysses, but I never met the right woman. I met a girl in Oklahoma thirty years ago but she went off with another fellow. Have you got it there, Walter?"

"Not yet," Mr. Covington said. "But I'll get it. I believe *this* is supposed to—no. Mr. Safferty *explained* how to get the animal out of the trap, but it seems I just can't get the hang of it. Maybe the principle changes when it's a small boy instead of an animal."

Two men, a woman with a small girl, and two boys of nine or ten came into the store to watch.

"What's the matter?" one of the boys said.

"We've got a boy caught in a trap here," Mr. Covington said. "A boy named Ulysses."

"How'd he get in?" one of the men said. "Shall I call a doctor?"

"No, he isn't hurt," Big Chris said. "The boy's all right. He's just off his feet, that's all."

"Maybe you ought to call the police," the woman said.

"No, lady," Big Chris said. "He's just caught in the trap. The man here—Walter—he'll get the boy out."

"Well," the lady said, "it's a shame the way little boys are made to suffer by all sorts of ridiculous mechanical devices."

"The boy's all right, lady," Big Chris said. "He *isn't* suffering."

"Well," the lady said, "if he were *my* boy, I'd have the police on you in two minutes." She turned away in a huff, dragging her little daughter along with her.

"I want to see, I want to see!" the little girl cried. "Everybody gets to see but *me!*" The woman turned and shook the little girl and dragged her out of the store.

"Now don't you worry, Ulysses," Big Chris said. "We'll get you out of this in no time at all."

Mr. Covington, however, gave up. "Maybe I'd better telephone Mr. Safferty," he said. "*I* can't get the boy out."

"Got to stay here?" Ulysses said.

"No, you don't, boy," Big Chris said. "No, you don't. We'll get you out."

A boy with a dozen afternoon papers under his arm came into the store, crowded into the scene, looked at Ulysses, looked at the people, looked at Ulysses again, and then spoke.

"Hello, Ulysses," he said. "What are you doing?"

"Hello, Auggie," Ulysses said. "Caught."

"What for?" Auggie said.

"Got caught," Ulysses said.

The newsboy tried to help Big Chris, but only got in the way. He looked around, panic-stricken and paralyzed, and after a moment of confusion bolted for the street. He ran straight to the telegraph office. Homer wasn't there, so he ran into the street again, running one way and then the other, bumping into people and shouting the day's headline all at the same time.

A woman who had been bumped said to herself, "Crazy!—Crazy from trying to sell papers!"

Auggie ran a full block, got out into the middle of the street to look around in four directions for Homer. It was a miracle that Homer appeared around a corner on his bicycle, but he did. Auggie ran toward Homer, shouting at him with all his might.

"Homer! You've got to come right away! Homer, you've got to—"

86

The Trap, My God, the Trap!

Homer got off his bicycle. "What's the matter, Auggie?" he said.

"Homer, something's happened!" Auggie shouted, even though Homer was right beside him. "You've got to come with me, Homer!" He took Homer by the arm.

"But what's the matter?" Homer said.

"Over at Covington's," Auggie said. "Hurry—you've got to come!"

"Ah," Homer said, "you want to show me some fishing tackle or a rifle or something in the window. I can't go around looking at things any more, Auggie. I'm working now. I've got to go to work."

Homer got back on his wheel and began to ride away, but Auggie took hold of the bike seat and trotted beside him, pushing the bike toward Covington's. "Homer," he shouted, "you've got to come with me! He's caught—he can't get out!"

"What are you talking about?" Homer said.

Now they were across the street from Covington's. There was a small crowd in front of the store, and Homer began to be a little frightened. Auggie pointed at the people. The two boys pushed through the crowd into the store, to the trap. There in the trap was Homer's brother Ulysses, and around the trap were Big Chris, Mr. Covington, and a number of strange men and women and boys.

"Ulysses!" Homer shouted.

"Hello, Homer," Ulysses said.

Homer turned to the people. "What's my brother doing in *that* thing?" he said.

"He got caught," Mr. Covington said.

"What are all these people doing around here?" Homer said. "Go on, go on home," he said to the people. "Can't a small boy get caught in a trap without the whole world hanging around?"

"Yes," Mr. Covington said, "I'll have to ask you people to go who are not customers." Mr. Covington studied the people. "Mr. Wallace," he said, "you can stay. You trade here, and you, Mr. Sickert. George. Mr. Spindle. Shorty."

"*I* trade here," a man said. "I bought fish hooks here not more than a week ago."

"Yes," Mr. Covington said, "fish hooks. The rest of you will have to go." Only two people moved away a little.

"Don't worry, Ulysses," Homer said. "Everything's going to be all right now. It's a good thing Auggie found me. Auggie, run over to the telegraph office and tell Mr. Spangler my brother Ulysses is caught in a trap at Covington's and I'm trying to get him out. I'm late already but tell him I'll be over as soon as I can get Ulysses out of the trap. Hurry now."

Auggie turned and ran. He bumped into a policeman who was coming into the store and almost knocked the man down.

"What's all the commotion about?" the policeman said.

The Trap, My God, the Trap!

"We've got a small boy caught in a trap here," Mr. Covington said. "Can't get him out."

"Let me look into this," the policeman said. He looked at Ulysses, and then turned to the people.

"All right now," he said, "get along with you, all of you. These things happen every day. You've got better things to do than stand around and watch a small boy in a trap." The policeman moved the people out of the store and locked the front door. He turned to Mr. Covington and Big Chris. "Now let's get this boy out of this thing and send him home," he said.

"Yes," Mr. Covington said, "and the sooner the better. You've got my shop closed at four-thirty in the afternoon."

"Well, how does this thing work?" Homer said.

"It's a new trap," Mr. Covington said—"just invented by Mr. Wilfred Safferty of Friant. He's asking twenty dollars for it and a patent's been applied for."

"Well, get my brother out of it," Homer said, "or get someone who *can*. Get Mr. Safferty."

"I've already tried to telephone Mr. Safferty but the telephone is out of order," Mr. Covington said.

"Out of order?" Homer shouted. He was very angry about the whole thing. "What do I care if the phone's out of order?" he said. "Get the man down here and get my brother out of the trap."

"Yes, I think you'd better do that," the policeman said to Mr. Covington.

"Officer," Mr. Covington said, "I'm trying to run a legitimate business. I'm a law-abiding citizen and I pay my taxes, out of which, I might say, you obtain your salary. I have already tried to reach Mr. Safferty by telephone. The telephone appears to be out of order. I cannot leave my shop in the middle of the day to go looking for him."

Homer looked Mr. Covington straight in the eye and placed a wagging finger under his nose. "You go get the inventor of this torture machine," he said, "and get my brother out of it. That's all."

"It's not a torture machine," Mr. Covington said. "It's the most improved animal trap on the market. It holds the animal aloft without damage to fur or body. No squeezing, cutting or crushing. It operates on the principle of dislocating the animal from its base and thereby rendering it powerless. Besides, Mr. Safferty may not be at home."

"Ah," Homer said, "what are you talking about?"

Now the policeman decided to study the trap. "Maybe," he suggested, "we'd better saw the boy out."

"Saw steel?" Mr. Covington said. "How?"

"Ulysses," Homer said, "do you want anything? Are you all right? Can I get you anything?"

Big Chris, sweating, working hard over the trap, looked from one brother to the other, deeply moved by the calm of the boy in the trap and the furious devotion of his brother.

"Ulysses." Homer said, "can I get you anything?"

"Papa," Ulysses said.

"Ah," Homer said, "can I get you anything besides Papa?"

"Marcus," the boy in the trap said.

"Marcus is in the Army," Homer said. "Do you want an ice cream cone or anything like that?"

"No," Ulysses said, "just Marcus."

"Well, Marcus is in the Army," Homer said. He turned to Covington. "Get my brother out of this thing and hurry up about it, too!" he said.

"Wait a minute," Big Chris said. "Hold your brother there, boy! Don't let him fall!" Big Chris was very busy with the trap now.

"You're *breaking* the trap!" Mr. Covington said. "It's the only one of its kind in the world. You mustn't break it! I'll go get Mr. Safferty. You're wrecking a great invention. Mr. Safferty's an old man. He may never be able to make another trap like this. The boy's all right. He's unhurt. I'll go get Mr. Safferty. I'll only be another hour or two."

"Another hour or two!" Homer shouted. He looked at Mr. Covington with the most terrible contempt in the world, and then all around at the store. "I'll break this whole store," he said. He turned to Big Chris. "Go ahead, mister," he said. "Break the trap—break it!"

Big Chris tugged at the trap with every muscle in his fingers, arms, shoulders and back, and little by little the trap began to give way to the force of his strength.

Ulysses twisted around to watch the man. At last Big Chris destroyed the trap.

Ulysses was free.

Holding him so that he would not fall on his face, Homer set his little brother on his feet. The crowd in front of the store cheered, but not effectively, as they were unorganized and had no leader. Ulysses tried out his legs. As everything seemed to be all right now, Homer put his arms around his brother. Ulysses looked at Big Chris. The big man was almost exhausted.

"Somebody's got to pay for that trap," Mr. Covington said. "It's ruined. Somebody's got to pay for it."

Without a word, Big Chris brought some currency out of his pocket, counted out twenty dollars of it and tossed it onto the counter. He took Ulysses by the head and rubbed the boy's hair, as a father sometimes does. Then he turned and walked out of the store.

Homer talked to his brother. "Are you all right?" he said. "How do you get into these terrible things?" Homer looked at the ruined trap and then kicked it.

"Careful there, boy," the policeman said. "That's some kind of a new invention. There's no telling what it's liable to do."

Mr. Covington went out into the street to speak to the people there. "The store is open for business again," he said. "Covington's opens at eight every morning, closes at seven every night, except Saturdays when we are open till ten. Closed all day Sunday. Everything in the sporting line. Fishing tackle, guns, ammunition, and athletic goods. We're open for business, ladies and gentlemen. Come right in."

The people slowly walked away.

Homer turned to the policeman before leaving the store. "Who was that man that got my brother out of the trap?" he said.

"Never saw the man before in my life," the policeman said.

"Big Chris," Ulysses said to Homer.

"Is that his name—Big Chris?" Homer said.

"Yes," Ulysses said. "Big Chris."

Now Auggie ran into the store. He looked at Ulysses. "Did you get out, Ulysses?" he said. "How did you get out, Ulysses?"

"Big Chris," Ulysses said.

"How did he get out, Homer?" Auggie said. "What happened? What happened to the trap? Where's the big man with the beard? What happened while I was gone?"

"Everything's all right, Auggie," Homer said. "Did you tell Mr. Spangler what I told you?"

"Yeah, I told him," Auggie said. "What happened, Homer? Does the trap work? Will it catch animals?"

"Ah," Homer said, "that trap's a lot of hooey. What good would it do you to catch an animal if you couldn't get it out? Mr. Covington," he said to the owner of the store, "you got a lot of nerve charging Big Chris twenty dollars for a piece of junk like that."

"Twenty dollars is the standard price," Mr. Covington said.

"Standard price?" Homer said. "What are you talking about? Come on, Auggie, let's get out of here." The three boys left the store and walked to the telegraph office. Mr. Spangler was leaning on the counter, looking out at the street. Mr. Grogan was sending a telegram. Homer was limping worse than ever now from his collision with Mr. Byfield in the two-twenty low hurdle race. He stopped to speak to the manager of the telegraph office.

"Mr. Spangler," he said, "this is my brother Ulysses. We just got him out of some kind of a trap over at Covington's. Big Chris got him out. He had to break the trap. And then he had to pay for it—twenty dollars. This is Auggie. Did he tell you why I'm late?"

"Everything's all right," Spangler said. "A few telegrams have piled up that you've got to deliver, but it's all right. So that's your brother—Ulysses?" Ulysses was standing behind the telegraph operator, watching him work. In front of the telegraph operator, across the table, Auggie stood, listening to the telegraph box.

"A few calls have come in, too," Spangler said. "I took a couple of the near ones myself. The other two are on the call sheet. Take the calls first, then deliver the telegrams."

The Trap, My God, the Trap!

"Yes, sir," Homer said. "Right away. I'm awfully sorry about this, Mr. Spangler. Will you mind Ulysses until I get back? Maybe a little later when things are quiet I can take him home on my wheel."

"I'll mind your brother," Spangler said. "You go ahead."

"Yes, sir," Homer said. "Thank you. Ulysses won't be any trouble. He'll just watch. He won't *do* anything."

Homer left the telegraph office, limping in a hurry.

CHAPTER 14

DIANA

Ulysses moved closer to Mr. Grogan while Auggie listened to the clatter of the telegraph box.

"What's that for?" Auggie said to Mr. Spangler, indicating the box.

"Mr. Grogan's sending a telegram," Spangler said.

"Where's he sending it to?" Auggie said.

"New York," Spangler said.

"All the way to New York?" Auggie said. "How does it go?"

"It goes by wire," Spangler said.

"Wires on telegraph poles?" Auggie said. "Telegraph poles from here to New York? All the way from Ithaca to New York?"

"That's right," Spangler said.

"Who sends them?" Auggie said.

"All sorts of people," Spangler said.

The newsboy thought a moment and then said, "I never got a telegram in my life. How do you get one?"

"Somebody sends you one," Spangler said.

"I never got any," Auggie said. "Who would send it?"

"Some friend or somebody," Spangler said.

"Everybody I know is right here in Ithaca," Auggie said. A green light went on, on the repeater rack. "What's that green light for?" Auggie said.

"It's a signal to us that the line is clear," Spangler said.

"What line?" Auggie said.

"The line to San Francisco," Spangler said.

"Oh," Auggie said. "How old do you have to be to be a messenger?"

"Sixteen," Spangler said.

"I'm nine," Auggie said. "What do you have to wait so long for? You can enlist in the Navy when you're seventeen."

"It's a rule," Spangler said.

"What have they got all them rules for all the time?" Auggie said.

Spangler began to file a batch of outgoing telegrams into a block of pigeonholes.

"Well," he said, "that rule is to keep children from working."

"Why?" Auggie said.

"So they won't get tired," Spangler said. "So they can play. That rule is for the protection of children."

"Protection from what?" Auggie said.

"Well," Spangler said, "protection from hard work, I guess. Protection from bosses who make kids do too much work for the money they're paid."

"Well, what if the kid doesn't want to be protected?" Auggie said. "What if he wants to work?"

"They protect him anyway," Spangler said.

"How old do you have to be not to be a child any more?" Auggie said. "How old do you have to be to be able to protect yourself, or to do any kind of work you want to do?"

"Got to be sixteen to be a messenger," Spangler said.

"Homer's working, isn't he?" Auggie said. "Since when is Homer sixteen?"

"Well," Spangler said, "Homer is an exception. He's only fourteen but he's strong and he's intelligent."

"What do you mean—intelligent?" Auggie said. "Do you have to be intelligent to be a messenger?"

"No," Spangler said, "but it helps. It helps to be intelligent no matter what you are."

"Well," Auggie said, "how can you tell if a man's intelligent?"

Spangler looked at the newsboy and smiled. "By talking to him a few minutes," he said.

"What are you putting those papers in there for?" Auggie said.

"These are telegrams that were sent yesterday," Spangler said. "We file them in here, city by city, for our records and our bookkeeping. Now this telegram is to San Francisco, so I put it in here. All these telegrams in here are to San Francisco."

"I can do that," Auggie said. "I can ride a bike, too—only I haven't got a bike. If I get a bike, Mr. Spangler, can I be a messenger too? Will you give me a job?"

Spangler stopped working to look at the boy. "Yes, I will, Auggie," he said, "but not just yet. Nine is not quite old enough. Thirteen or fourteen —yes."

"Twelve maybe?" Auggie said.

"Maybe," Spangler said. "What do you want to be a messenger for?"

"Learn things," Auggie said. "Read telegrams. Find out about things." He paused a moment. "I won't be twelve for three years," he said.

"Three years will go by in no time at all," Spangler said.

"Doesn't seem like it," Auggie said. "I've been waiting a long time already."

"You'll find out," Spangler said. "You'll be twelve before you know it. What's your last name?"

"Gottlieb," Auggie said. "August Gottlieb."

The manager of the telegraph office and the news-boy looked at each other, each of them very earnest and very serious. "August Gottlieb," Spangler said, "I give you my word. When the time comes—"

Spangler stopped speaking to behold a young woman named Diana Steed galloping into the office. In front of the office in the street was the automobile which had brought her. At the wheel of the automobile sat a chauffeur in uniform. In a special, somewhat artificial yet attractive voice, she cried out to Spangler, "Oh, there you are, darling!" She charged upon him with a sweet fury of affection, threw her arms around him, and kissed him in a way that was so incredible it might have been real, or a little better than real.

"Wait a minute!" Spangler said. He held her back, put the wire basket he was holding on the desk, and turned to her. The young woman came for him again but he warded her off. "Wait a minute," he said. "This is August Gottlieb!"

"How do you do, little boy?" the young woman said.

"August," Spangler said, "this is Miss Steed."

"Hello," Auggie said. And then, not knowing what else to say, he said, "Paper, lady?"

"Why, yes, of course," Diana said. "How much is it?"

"Five cents," Auggie said. "Home edition. Race results, stock market closings, and the latest news of the War."

"Yes?" Diana said. "Here's a nickel. Thank you very much."

Auggie took the nickel and gave Miss Steed a paper which he first folded in a very efficient and businesslike way, whacking the full paper on his knee, folding it in half, whacking the half paper on his knee, folding that in half, and then, turning the result around neatly, somewhat like a magician doing an important trick, he handed it to her. "Thank you, ma'am," he said. "Wednesdays I sell *The Saturday Evening Post* and *Liberty*. Fridays, *Collier's*. I work the whole town."

"Well," Diana said, "I hope you make a lot of money, little boy."

"I average about forty cents a day, papers and magazines both," Auggie said. "When the County Fair opens I sell soda pop."

"Well, you *do* keep busy, *don't* you?" Diana said in her wonderful cheerful voice.

"Yes," Auggie said, "and I learn things, too. I can figure people out pretty good." It appeared that Auggie had figured Miss Steed out and was pleased with the results.

"Yes, you do," she said, "I'm sure you do." She turned to Spangler. "I waited for your call, darling," she said. "You *did* say you would call at five, didn't you?"

"Oh, yeah," Spangler said. "I forgot. I was talking to Auggie here. He wants to be a messenger and

I've just told him when the time comes he's going to have a job."

"Well, thanks, Mr. Spangler," Auggie said. He moved to go. "I'll be seeing you," he said. "Good-by, ma'am." He turned to the little boy. "Good-by, Ulysses," he said.

"Ulysses!" Diana said to Spangler. "My, what a refreshing name! Ulysses! Ulysses in Ithaca! Darling, I've only a moment. You will be out for dinner, won't you? You *must*, you know."

Spangler began to speak but the young woman stopped him. "No," she said, "you promised! Yes, you did! Mother and Father are dying to meet you! Seven o'clock sharp!"

"Now wait a minute," Spangler said. "Wait a minute."

"Darling," Diana said, "you can't disappoint me again, can you?"

"Nothing in the world is ever going to disappoint *you*," Spangler said, "so take it easy. Seven o'clock sharp? What do you mean—sharp? What do you want me to come to dinner for?"

"Because I love you, darling," the young woman said very patiently, as if Spangler were a child. "I love you, love you, love you, do you hear?" she said, laughing cheerfully.

"Now take it easy," the manager of the telegraph office said. "Every time you come out with that kind of talk I—"

"But I *do* love you, darling," the young woman said earnestly.

Spangler sighed. "I've been out to dinner twice in my life," he said. "I was bored both times."

"You'll like Mother and Father," Diana said. "We're not dressing—just evening clothes."

"What do you mean—evening clothes?" Spangler said. "I'm wearing the clothes I wear day and evening both."

"Seven o'clock," Diana said. She noticed the hard-boiled egg on Spangler's desk. "Oh, darling," she said, "what a clever paper weight! What is it?"

"It's an egg," Spangler said. "A real egg. I keep it for luck."

"How sweet!" Diana said. "Well, darling, I've got to run." She moved toward him for a farewell kiss but he warded her off gently and she left the office.

Mr. Grogan finished typing a telegram. Spangler led Ulysses over to the old man. "Willie," he said, "I'm going over to Corbett's for a drink. This is Ulysses Macauley, Homer's little brother. He's had an experience of some sort. Got caught in some kind of trap. Ulysses, this is Mr. Willie Grogan."

"Oh, we're old friends," Mr. Grogan said. "He's been watching me work." Ulysses nodded.

"One minute and I'll be right back," Spangler said.

CHAPTER 15

THE GIRL ON THE CORNER

Spangler turned to go, but he was stopped by the working of the call box—by the message which simultaneously rang out and printed itself upon the ticker tape. He went to the instrument on the delivery desk and studied the marks on the tape. "That's a call from Ithaca Wine," he said to Grogan—"away out in the sticks. If Homer comes in, keep him here until we get the regular evening call from Sunripe Raisin. He's beat Western Union there twice in two tries. If he can make it again today we may have a pretty good month of business after all. How many did we get yesterday?"

The Girl on the Corner

"Sixty-seven," Grogan said.

"Sixty-seven telegrams out of sixty-eight," Spangler said. "First boy there gets all the telegrams but one. Second boy gets one. Well, I'll go over to Corbett's."

But now another call began to come in: *Dot dot dash dot dot dot.* When the manager of the telegraph office had heard only the first two dots, he knew the call was from Sunripe Raisin, and as Homer was not in the office to take the call, he shouted to Grogan, *"I'll* take the call. I'll get there first myself."

By the time the call was repeated three times, Spangler was in the middle of the next block, moving through the people like an open field runner in a football game. On the corner before him, thirty yards away, stood a shy, lonely-looking girl of eighteen or nineteen—tired, sweet, hushed, and wonderful. She was waiting for a bus to take her home, after work. Even though he was running, it was impossible for Spangler not to notice the girl's loneliness —which seemed to him, even though he was in a hurry, like the loneliness of *all* things. Not clowning, without any premeditation, swiftly and easily, he reached the girl, paused a moment, and kissed her on the cheek. Before he moved on, he told the girl the only thing it was possible to say to her: "You are the loveliest woman in the world!"

He ran on. When he was going up the steps of

the Sunripe Raisin Association three at a time, the Western Union messenger, off to a slow start because the delivery clerk did not know the calls by heart as Spangler did, was just getting off his bicycle in front of the building, and when Spangler was going into the office, the Western Union messenger had only begun to wait for the elevator.

As if he were still a messenger, Spangler announced himself to the old woman at the desk of Sunripe Raisin. "Postal Telegraph!" he said.

"Tom!" the old woman said, pleased and surprised. "Don't tell me you're a *messenger* now, too."

"Once a messenger, always a messenger," Spangler said, not at all embarrassed by the meaninglessness of the remark. He smiled at the old woman and then said, "But most of all I came to see *you*, Mrs. Brockington."

The Western Union messenger came into the office. "Western Union," he said.

"Well, Harry," Mrs. Brockington said, "you've been beaten again." She handed the messenger one telegram. "Better luck next time," she said.

The Western Union boy, a little confused and embarrassed because he had been beaten again, this time not by another messenger but by the manager of the Postal Telegraph office, took the one telegram and said, "Thanks just the same, Mrs. Brockington," and left the office.

The old woman handed Spangler a whole bundle of telegrams. "Here you are, Tom," she said, "one hundred and twenty-nine night letters—all over the country—all paid."

"One hundred and twenty-nine?" Spangler said. "That's going to give me a good month of business after all." He leaned over the railing and kissed the old woman.

"Now, Tom!" Mrs. Brockington said.

"No," Spangler said, "you mustn't be unkind to me. I've been wanting to kiss you ever since I first came in here and saw you—remember? Twenty years —and you've become more beautiful every year."

"Now, Tom," the old woman said, "don't you be teasing an old woman."

"Old?" Spangler said. "Not *you!*"

"You're sweet, Tom," Mrs. Brockington said, "and so are all your messengers—but where is the new one?"

"Homer?" Spangler said. "You mean Homer Macauley? You'll be seeing him every day—*first,* too. We got slowed down this afternoon on account of an accident that happened to his little brother, a boy named Ulysses. Got caught in some kind of a trap at Covington's. Homer had to go and get him out. But you'll be seeing him from now on." He stopped and smiled at the old woman. "Good night, Emily," he said.

"How sweet of you to remember my name," the old woman said.

In the street he felt very good—about everything

—about Homer getting Ulysses out of the trap, about Grogan being able to do his work even though he had long since passed the pension age, about Ulysses standing around being fascinated by everything in the telegraph office, about Auggie wanting to grow up swiftly and be a messenger, about Diana Steed, even. But most of all he felt happy about the girl who had been waiting for the bus on the street corner. When he reached the place where the girl had stood, he paused a moment. He said to himself, "It was right here that she was standing. I'll never see her again most likely, but even if I do, I'll never see her again as she was when I saw her this afternoon." He moved on down the street, whistling to himself. When he was across the street from Corbett's, he heard pianola music—the old waltz called *All That I Want Is You*. He moved to the swinging doors of the place, listened a moment, then went on in. Corbett himself was standing there and immediately went to work, getting Spangler his regular drink.

"Hello, Ralph," Spangler said. "How's it going?" He glanced over at the three soldiers listening to the player piano.

"Not bad, not good," Corbett said. "Soldiers with a lot of time to kill and not very much money. I buy them three to their one, and when they're broke and ready to go I give them back their money. Why not?"

"Can you afford to do that?" Spangler said.

The Girl on the Corner

"No," Corbett said, "but what's the difference? After the War maybe I'll get some of it back. I just can't be a waiter. I'm Young Corbett." He stopped a moment to remember something that was troubling him.

"Last night, Tom," he said, "I'm tending bar, trying to get along, and a wise guy calls out to me, 'Hey, screwball! Get me another drink.' He wasn't a soldier. He was somebody from Ithaca. Well, I look around—nobody else behind the bar—just me. 'Screwball? Are you talking to *me?*' I tell him. 'I ain't talking to myself, screwball,' the guy says. Well, what am I going to do? I can't hit the guy because I've been in the ring. I went over to him and took him—like *this.*" Corbett took Spangler by the coat lapel with one hand, and with the other, lifted high, palm open, he waited a furious moment. Then he said what he had said the night before to the bad drinker: "You're talking to Young Corbett. If I *slap* you, you'll probably fall down and die, and I don't want anybody to die in my place. Now get out of here and don't come back. Don't ever step into this joint again as long as you live. And when you go out, be glad you're alive."

Corbett let go of Spangler's coat. He was trembling with rage. "My hands were shaking all night after that," he said, "but last night wasn't the first time something like that happened. It happens almost every night. And every time it happens I tell myself, 'No more! I've got to close the place. Got to get away.' I'm getting scared. Some night I'm afraid I'm going to lose my head and murder somebody. Running a bar isn't an easy thing. I've got too good a heart to be a bartender."

The manager of the telegraph office and the former prize fighter talked along for another five minutes and then Spangler went back to the office. As he left the place, the soldiers had the player piano going strong. Now the song was *White Blossom*. The soldiers watched the words as they moved down the roll and tried to sing with the piano music. Spangler listened a moment. Their singing wasn't particularly good, but the feeling with which they sang was not bad at all.

CHAPTER 16

I'LL TAKE YOU HOME AGAIN

Thomas Spangler, manager of the Postal Telegraph office of Ithaca, California, walked into his office. At the delivery desk he saw the Macauley brothers, Homer and Ulysses—the messenger folding telegrams and putting them in envelopes, the younger brother watching with quiet admiration. The messenger turned to his boss.

"Did *you* get Sunripe Raisin, Mr. Spangler?" he said.

"Yes, I did," Spangler said. "One hundred and twenty-nine telegrams." He showed the telegrams to the messenger.

"One hundred and twenty-nine!" Homer said "How did you get there first?"

"I ran," Spangler said.

"You beat Western Union to Sunripe Raisin *running?*" Homer said.

"Sure," Spangler said. "Nothing to it. I even stopped on the way—to pay tribute to beauty and innocence." Homer didn't understand, but Spangler went right on. "No, no, I won't explain it," Spangler said. "Take Ulysses home."

"Yes, sir," Homer said. "We've got a call from Guggenheim's. It's down our way, so I'll hike Ulysses home, then go to Guggenheim's and from there I'll go to Ithaca Wine, then Foley's, and then I'll come right back. I'll be back in no time at all." The messenger left the office and carefully set his brother on the handlebars of his bicycle while Spangler watched. The older brother swung onto the bike and began to pedal down the street. When they were out of the town itself, Ulysses twisted around to look at his brother. For the first time that day his face broke out with the Macauley smile.

"Homer?" he said.

"What do you want?" Homer said.

"I can sing," Ulysses said.

"That's good," Homer said.

Ulysses began to sing. "We will sing one song," he sang. He stopped and began again. "We will sing one song," he sang again, but he stopped again and immediately began again. "We will sing one song."

"That's not a song, Ulysses," Homer said. "That's only a little part of a song. Now you listen to me, and then sing with me." The older brother began to sing while the younger brother listened.

"Weep no more, my lady. O weep no more today
We will sing one song for the old Kentucky home
For the old Kentucky home far away"

"Sing it again, Homer," Ulysses said.

"O.K.," Homer said, and began the song again, but this time the younger brother sang with the older, and as they sang Ulysses saw the freight train again with the Negro leaning over the side of the gondola, smiling and waving. That was one of the most wonderful things that had ever happened to Ulysses Macauley in his four years of life in the world. He waved to a man and the man waved back to *him*—not once, but many times. He would remember that as long as he lived.

Homer got off his bicycle in front of the Macauley house and carefully set Ulysses on his feet. They stood together a moment, listening to the harp and piano of their mother and sister and the singing of their neighbor, Mary Arena.

"All right, Ulysses," Homer said, "you're home now. Go on in. Mama's there, and Bess and Mary. I've got to go on to work."

"Going to work?" Ulysses said.

"Yes," Homer said, "but I'll be home tonight. Go on in, Ulysses." The younger brother started up the front porch steps. When he got to the door, the older brother began to ride on down the street.

CHAPTER 17

THREE SOLDIERS

When the Steed family and their guests, including Thomas Spangler, sat down to dinner, a heavy rain was falling over Ithaca. Bess Macauley and Mary Arena, in raincoats and galoshes, walked to the telegraph office, bearing Homer's lunch-box. As they passed the Owl Drug Store, a young man standing in the doorway gave them the old wolf eye.

"Hi-ya, pretty," he said to Bess. "What's with?"

Bess ignored the young man and moved closer to Mary as they went up the street. Now, coming toward them were three young soldiers. They were sporting around in the street at a game improvised out of their happiness at being free for the night, out of the noble and ridiculous world and its constant comedy, and out of the refreshing rain. They pushed and chased one another, roaring with uncontrollable laughter, and calling out the nicknames they had given one another—Fat, Texas, and Horse. When the three boys saw Mary and Bess they came to a worshipful halt. They bowed very low, one after another. The girls were pleased, but they weren't sure what they ought to do—what attitude they ought to take.

"They're just soldiers, Bess," Mary whispered—"away from home."

"Let's stop," Bess said.

The two girls stopped to face the three soldiers.

The one called Fat stepped forward as the official representative of the group—the soldiers' ambassador to American girls.

"My ladies," he said, "we of the great Democratic Army, your humble servants, the soldiers—here today and, we hope, here tomorrow—thank you for your beautiful faces, in times of dryness no less than in times of rain, such as the present. May I present my comrades and your devoted admirers. This is Texas—he's from New Jersey. This is Horse—he's from Texas. And I'm Fat—I'm from hunger. Now more than anything else I hunger for the companionship of beautiful American girls. How about it?"

"Well," Bess said, "we were going to the Kinema."

"To the Kinema!" Fat said dramatically. "May we—soldiers—whether here today or gone tomorrow—accompany you—American girls—to the Kinema? Tonight is tonight and tomorrow is tomorrow, but tomorrow we return to barracks, to the awful but necessary business of war, to the holy work of destroying the murderous microbe in man which seeks to crush man's free spirit. Tonight we are your brothers—far from our own firesides, and lonely. Yes, although happy and proud, we *are* lonely, for Ithaca is not our native land. I have waddled into this costume of the American soldier from the side streets of that ferocious city Chicago, of that sweet nation Illinois. Restore me to that city and to that nation tonight in memory, and restore my good brothers each to his good place. Consider with generous hearts our humble petition, for we are of one family, the human, and except for war we might never meet. This moment is by the gentler centuries made." The soldier who was called Fat bowed, then stood upright. "What is your decision?" he said.

"Is he crazy?" Mary whispered.

"No," Bess said, "he's just lonely. Let's go to the movie with them."

"All right, Bess," Mary said, "but you *tell* him. I don't know what to say."

Bess turned to the soldier. "All right," she said.

"Thank you, ladies," the soldier called Fat said. "Thank you." He offered his arm to Bess. "Shall we go, then?" he said.

"First I've got to take my brother his lunch-box," Bess said. "He works at the telegraph office. It won't take a minute."

"Telegraph?" the soldier called Fat said. "Then I shall send a telegram." He turned to the others. "How about you, Texas?"

"How much does it cost to send a telegram to New Jersey?" Texas said.

"Not nearly as much as it's worth," Fat said. He turned to the other soldier. "Horse?"

"Yeah," the soldier called Horse said. "I think I'd like to send a telegram to Ma and Joe and Kitty —that's my girl," he said to Bess.

"Every girl in the world is *my* girl," Fat said, "and as I cannot send telegrams to each of them, I shall send a telegram to only one. I shall send millions of telegrams in the one telegram."

Willie Grogan, the old telegraph operator, was alone in the office when the two young women and the three soldiers walked in. The old man stood behind the counter.

"I'm Homer's sister Bess," Bess said. "I've brought his lunch." She put the box on the counter.

"How do you do, Miss Macauley," Grogan said. "Homer will be in soon. I'll see that he gets his lunch."

"And these boys want to send telegrams," Bess said.

"Very well, young men," Grogan said. "Telegraph blanks and pencils."

"How much does it cost to send a telegram to Jersey City?" Texas said.

"Twenty-five words for fifty cents," Grogan said, "plus a small tax. But don't count the address or the signature. The telegram will be delivered tomorrow morning."

"Fifty cents?" Texas said. "That's not bad at all." He began to write his telegram.

"How much does it cost to San Antone?" Horse said.

"Half as much as to Jersey City," Grogan said. "San Antonio is nearer Ithaca than Jersey City."

The soldier called Fat who had been busy writing his telegram now handed it to the old man. Grogan read the telegram as he counted it.

EMMA DANA
C/O THE UNIVERSITY OF CHICAGO
CHICAGO, ILLINOIS

MY DARLING, I LOVE YOU, I MISS YOU, I THINK OF YOU ALWAYS. KEEP WRITING. THANKS FOR THE SWEATER. I AM LEARNING REAL POLITICAL ECONOMY NOW. WE WILL BE GOING INTO ACTION SOON. DON'T FORGET TO GO TO CHAPEL SUNDAY AND PRAY FOR US. I AM HAPPY. I LOVE YOU.

NORMAN

Next, the soldier called Texas handed Grogan *his* telegram.

MRS. EDITH ANTHONY
1702½ WILMINGTON STREET
JERSEY CITY, NEW JERSEY

DEAR MA. HOW ARE YOU? I AM FINE. I GOT YOUR LETTER AND THE BOX OF DRIED FIGS. THANKS. DON'T WORRY ABOUT ANYTHING. SO LONG. LOVE.

BERNARD

Then, the soldier called Horse handed the old telegraph operator *his* telegram.

MRS. HARVEY GUILFORD
211 SANDYFORD BOULEVARD
SAN ANTONIO, TEXAS

HELLO MA. JUST WANT TO SAY HELLO FROM ITHACA IN SUNNY CALIFORNIA. ONLY IT'S RAINING. HA HA. GIVE MY REGARDS TO EVERYBODY. TELL JOE HE CAN HAVE MY GUN AND SHELLS. DON'T FORGET TO WRITE.

QUENTIN

The soldiers and the girls left the office and Mr. Grogan went to his table to send the telegrams.

On the screen at the Kinema Theatre, as the three soldiers and the two American girls walked down the center aisle, Mr. Winston Churchill, Prime Minister of England in the year of our Lord 1942, appeared before the Canadian House of Parliament. By the time the young people were seated, Mr. Churchill had said three things, one after another, which had caused increasing delight both to the members of the Canadian House of Parliament and to the members of the audience at the Kinema

Theatre in Ithaca. The soldier called Fat leaned over to Bess Macauley.

"There," he said, "is one of the great men of our time—and a great American, too."

"I thought Churchill was an Englishman," the soldier called Horse said.

"Sure," Fat said, "but he's an American, too. From now on every good man in the world is going to be an American." He moved just a little closer to the girl on the other side of him, Mary Arena. "Thanks a lot for letting us come to the movie with you," he said. "It feels better to have girls near. It smells better than just soldiers."

"We were coming to the movie anyway," Mary said.

Now the man named Franklin Delano Roosevelt, President of the United States, appeared in the newsreel, making a radio speech to the nation from his home in Hyde Park. He spoke with his usual mixture of solemnity and humor. The five young people listened carefully and the whole audience applauded when the speech was ended.

"There's the greatest American of them all," the soldier called Horse said. At that moment the American flag appeared on the screen and a good portion of the audience began to applaud.

"And there," the soldier called Texas said, "is the greatest flag in the world."

"I don't know—," the soldier called Fat said to Bess. —"A man doesn't begin to really love his country until it's in trouble. All the rest of the time he takes it for granted—like his family."

"I get a lump in my throat every time I see the flag," Bess said. "It used to make me think of Washington and Lincoln, but now it makes me think of my brother Marcus. He's a soldier, too."

"Oh, you've got a brother in the Army?" Fat said.

"Yes," Bess said. "He was somewhere in North Carolina the last time we heard from him."

"Well," Fat said, "I guess the flag makes every person think of what's nearest and most precious to him. It makes *me* think of Chicago—and that means everything in it—everything good and everything bad, too. My family—my girl—they're good. And the slums and politics—they're bad—but I love them all. We'll get rid of the slums some day, and the politics, too."

"I don't suppose we have slums in Ithaca," Bess said—"just poor people. I guess we've got some kind of city government, but I don't suppose we've got much politics to speak of. Our family doesn't bother much about things like that, anyway. We like music. I just bet my brother Marcus is playing the accordion somewhere right now."

Her brother Marcus was at that moment at a bar in a cafe now called The Dive Bomber in a small town in North Carolina. His friend Tobey George and three other soldiers were at the bar with him. Marcus was playing the song called *A Dream*, and Tobey was singing. Two soldiers danced in the place with two girls, not unlike Mary and Bess. After the song, Tobey sat down beside his friend Marcus and asked him to talk some more about Ithaca and the Macauleys there.

As Marcus Macauley began to tell Tobey George about Ithaca, Thomas Spangler and Diana Steed came down the aisle of the Kinema Theatre. Now, the feature picture began to appear on the screen. When they were seated the screen was filling with words, not pictures. These words named the picture and the people who had helped to make the picture. There were vast numbers of words, an enormous amount of credit given to enormous numbers of people. Accompanying these credits was a majestically inappropriate theme of music which had been especially composed for the occasion.

Spangler and Diana sat very close to the screen, in the third row, ten rows in front of Bess and Mary and the three soldiers. Their seats were at the very center of a row whose only other occupants were small boys. Now on the screen appeared the spick and span linoleum-floored hall of a hospital. Over a loud-speaker at the end of the hall came the harsh voice of a bitter nurse who spoke over-emphatically.

"Dr. Cavanagh!" she cried. "Surgery! Dr. Cavanagh! Surgery!"

Immediately upon hearing these words Thomas Spangler got to his feet. He had had a few to drink and the evening had been a rather important and pleasant one for him, full of troubles which were now working themselves out, it seemed, so that he felt no need at all not to carry on as if he himself were no older than the others in that row of seats.

"Ooop!" he said. "Wrong movie!" He took Diana's hand and said, "Come on."

"But, darling, the movie isn't over yet!" the young woman whispered.

Spangler dragged her along. "It's over for *me*," he said. "Come on." Now they were passing a small boy who was watching the screen with great fascination.

"*You'll* get to Heaven," Spangler said to the boy, and then to Diana, "Come on, come on, don't stand in the boy's way."

"But, darling," Diana said, "the movie's just beginning."

Now the boy spoke to Spangler. "What did you say, mister?" he said.

"Heaven!—Heaven!" Spangler said. "I say you'll get there."

The boy wasn't sure he understood what Spangler meant. "Have you got the time?" he said.

"No, I haven't," Spangler said, "but it's still early."

"Yes, sir," the boy said.

Now Spangler and the young woman were walking up the aisle of the movie theater.

"Let's stop on the way," Spangler said. "Have a cup of coffee, listen to the pianola, and then you can go home." He turned in order to face the screen and began walking backward.

"Look at Dr. Cavanagh, will you?" he said. "He's going to do something with that pair of pliers. Probably get confused and pull out one of his front teeth. Look at him!"

In the lobby of the theater the young woman did not mind so much leaving the picture so soon after its beginning. "You do love me, don't you?" she said to Spangler. "Yes, you do. You know you do."

"Love you?" Spangler almost shouted. "I took you to a movie, didn't I?"

They went on out to the street and began hurrying on their way, moving close to the buildings in order to keep out of the rain.

CHAPTER 18

MR. GROGAN ON WAR

As Spangler and Diana ran through the rain toward Corbett's, Homer Macauley, soaking wet, brought his bicycle to a stop in front of the telegraph office and went in. He looked over the situation at the delivery desk. There were no calls to take, but there was one telegram to deliver.

Mr. Grogan finished a telegram he was typing and got up. "Your sister Bess brought your lunch, boy," he said.

"She did?" Homer said. "Ah, she didn't need to bring any lunch. I was going to get us two pies." He took the box and said, "There's *enough* of it. Will you have some lunch with me, Mr. Grogan?"

"Thank you, boy," the old telegraph operator said. "I'm not hungry."

"Maybe if you start to eat a little," Homer said, "your appetite will improve, Mr. Grogan."

"No," the old man said, "thanks very much. But you're soaking wet. Look here, we've got raincoats."

"Yeah," Homer said, "but I got *caught* in the rain." Homer bit into a sandwich. "I'll eat this one sandwich," he said, "and then I'll deliver the telegram." He chewed a moment and then looked over at the old telegraph operator. "What kind of a telegram is it?" he said.

Mr. Grogan didn't answer, so that Homer knew the telegram was another death message. He stopped chewing and gulped the food down dry. "I wish I didn't have to deliver telegrams like this," the messenger said to the telegraph operator.

"I know," Mr. Grogan said slowly. He didn't speak again for half a minute, while the messenger held the unfinished sandwich in his hand without taking another bite. "Go ahead, boy," Mr. Grogan said, "eat your lunch. Your sister was with another girl—a very pretty girl."

"Oh, that's Mary," Homer said. "She's our neighbor. She's Marcus's girl. My brother—in the Army. They're going to be married after the War."

"Your sister and Mary were with three soldiers who sent telegrams," the old telegraph operator said.

"Is that so?" Homer said. "Where are the telegrams?"

Mr. Grogan indicated the hook on which dispatched telegrams were placed. Homer took the telegrams off the hook and one by one read them. After having read them, he looked up at the old telegraph operator.

"If a fellow dies that way, Mr. Grogan," the messenger said, "somebody you know, or somebody you don't know, somebody you've never even seen—does it make anything better? This is only Ithaca. This is only *one* little town in America. These telegrams go everywhere, to rich people and poor people, to every kind of people there is. What about these people? They don't just die for nothing, do they?"

The old telegraph operator waited a moment before speaking, and then, as if there was so much to say that he wouldn't be able to make it alone, he went to the drawer of his table and got out his bottle. He took a good long swig, sat down, and looked over at the messenger.

"I've been a long time in the world," he said. "Too long perhaps. Let me tell you that in war or in peace, nothing is for nothing—least of all dying. The old man stopped a moment to take another swig. "All people are one," he said, "as you are one. Now, as there is mischief in you along with good, there is mischief and good in *all* people. It is mixed in all of them, the millions of them of all nations. Yes, *our* nation, too. As a man's conscience struggles with the opposites in his own nature, so do these opposites struggle in the whole body of the living—in the whole world. And that is when we have a war. The body is fighting off its diseases. But don't you worry about it, because the good endures forever and the evil is driven away every time it appears. The sick body and the sick spirit are always restored to health. They may take sick again but they will always get better, and as each fresh disease comes and is driven off, the body and spirit strengthen until at last they are powerful, as they were meant to be, cleansed of all decay, refined, gentler, nobler, and beyond corruption. Every man in the world, right or wrong, is trying." The old man was a little weary now. "The thief and the murderer are trying," he sighed. "Nobody dies for *nothing*. They die seeking grace, seeking to be immortal, seeking truth and justice—and one day that great body of man— all of us, every last one of us—shall reach home, shall have grace, shall be immortal, and this wonderful evil world shall be a place of decency and goodness among men."

The old man sighed deeper than ever now and then after a moment brought out a small slip of paper from his vest pocket. He handed the paper to the messenger. "Will you go on an errand for me again," he said, "to the drug store?"

"Yes, sir," Homer said, and hurried out of the office.

William Grogan stood alone in the telegraph office, looking around with a strange affection for everything, mixed with a kind of loving fury. Almost slowly he clutched his heart as if he had been waiting patiently for the swift attack which no longer could surprise him. He moved back to his chair and sat in a terrible stiffness until the attack had spent its most extreme energy.

The messenger returned from the drug store and handed the telegraph operator the small box.

"Water," the old man said.

Homer filled a paper cup full of water and took it to the old man, who dumped three of the pills out of the little box, tossed them into his mouth, took the cup from Homer, and swallowed the pills.

"Thank you," he said, "thank you, my boy."

"Yes, sir," Homer said.

He looked at the old man a moment to see if he was going to be all right, then went to the delivery desk and took up the telegram of death. He stood a moment holding the telegram and looking at it, and then he opened the envelope and took the message out of it, to read. He put the telegram back into a new envelope, sealed it, and then turned and walked out of the office into the rain. The old telegraph operator got up out of his chair and followed the boy into the street. He stood there on the sidewalk and watched the boy push against the wind and the rain. Inside the office the telegraph box began to rattle, but the old man didn't hear. The telephone rang, but again the old man didn't hear. He did not turn and go back into the office until the telephone had rung seven times.

CHAPTER 19

TO MOTHER, WITH LOVE

Fifteen minutes later Homer Macauley got off his
bicycle in front of a large fine old house where a
party was in progress. Through the windows the
messenger could see four young couples dancing,
and as he was sure everybody inside the house was
happy, the boy felt sick and terrified. He went to
the door of the house and stood a moment, listening
to the music. He moved a finger toward the door
bell and then let his hand drop.

"I'll go back to the office," he said to himself
aloud. "I'll quit. I don't want a job like this."

He sat down on the steps of the house. After a

long time he got up and went to the door and pressed his finger against the button. When the door opened he saw a young woman, and before he knew what he was doing he turned and ran to his bicycle. The young woman came out on the porch of the house and called out, "Why, what's the matter, boy?"

Homer got off his bicycle and walked to the porch slowly. "I'm sorry," he said to the young woman. "I've got a telegram for Mrs. Claudia Beaufrere."

"It's Mother's birthday," the young woman said cheerfully. She turned and stepped into the hallway of the house. "Mother," she called out, "here's a telegram for you."

The girl's mother came to the door. "It's from Alan, I'm sure," she said. "Come in, young man," she said to Homer. "You must have a piece of my birthday cake."

"No, thank you, ma'am," Homer said. "I've got to go back to work." He held the telegram out to the woman, who took it as if it were nothing more than a birthday greeting.

"Nonsense," she said cheerfully—"not until you've had a piece of cake and a glass of punch." She tugged at Homer's arm and dragged him into the room to a table loaded with cake and sandwiches and punch. The music and dancing continued. "It's my birthday, boy," the woman said. "Lord," she laughed, "I *am* old. Well, you must wish me happiness, boy." She handed Homer a glass of punch.

"I wish you—" Homer began to say. He stopped, and then began again. "I wish you—" But he couldn't go on. He put the glass of punch on the table and bolted to the door. The mother looked around the room, then went to one side where she wouldn't be noticed, and the daughter, watching the mother, moved to the other side. Homer was on his bicycle hurrying through the rain back to the telegraph office. On the wall of the hall, in front of the mother, was a framed picture of a good-looking red-headed boy. Written on the photograph were the words, "To Mother with love from Alan on his 12th birthday." The mother opened the telegram, read it, and without a sound began to sob, while the phonograph continued with a song called *Chanson pour Ma Brune,* and the happy people continued to dance. The daughter looked across the room at her mother in the hallway. Almost as if she had lost her reason, she rushed to the phonograph and turned it off.

"Mother!" the girl cried, and ran toward the woman in the hallway.

CHAPTER 20

IT'S YOUR MISFORTUNE
AND NONE OF MY OWN

Now, the Kinema Theatre was letting out its visitors after the last show. In the street Bess turned to the soldier called Fat and said, "Well, we must go home now."

"Thank you, ladies," the soldier called Fat said. It was time for them to say good-by, and yet somehow they stood together in the street, waiting, as if something wonderful but unknowable was on the verge of happening. The soldier called Fat looked from Bess to Mary, and then very easily and innocently kissed Bess and then Mary.

Now, the soldier called Horse shouted, "Well, what about us? What about me and Texas? We're somebody, too. We're in the Army, too." So this soldier kissed Bess and Mary, too. And after him Texas kissed them. A woman in the street watched with bitter distaste. The girls turned quickly and hurried down the street. The soldier called Horse jumped, and then pushed the soldier called Texas, who turned and pushed the soldier called Fat. They moved down the side street, shouting at one another.

"Waaa-hooo! Oh you Texas! Oh you Fat!" Horse shouted.

"How you talk, boy!" Texas shouted to Fat. "How you talk! Old Senator Fat from the University of Chicago!"

The soldier called Fat cackled with delight as they moved on down the dark street, pushing and laughing and shouting.

"Oh man!" the soldier called Fat shouted. "When I get to Congress! I'll tell them a thing or two."

"Yippee-aye-ay," Horse shouted. *"Git along little dogies—it's your misfortune and none of my own."*

Now the three soldiers began leaping over one another at a swift, crazy game of leap-frog, pushing down the dark, immortal street nearer and nearer to the War.

CHAPTER 21

A BETTER WORLD, A
BETTER PEOPLE

By the time the unhappy messenger got back to
the telegraph office from the Beaufrere home, the
rain had stopped, the moon was shining, and an
empty and exhausted cluster of clouds, now white,
was being driven across the sky. The messenger was
very tired when he came limping into the office.

"What's the matter with your leg, boy?" the old
telegraph operator said. "You've been limping all
day."

"It's nothing," Homer said. "Any more telegrams?"

"All clear," Mr. Grogan said, "and soon you can go home to bed. Now tell me. What happened to your leg?"

"I guess I twisted a ligament or broke it, or something," Homer said. He tried his leg out. "I was running the two-twenty low hurdles," he said. "The coach out at Ithaca High School never did like me, I guess. I was running first when he came out to the track and tried to stop me—it was my own fault, I guess. I saw him coming and I could have stopped if I had wanted to, but I *didn't* want to. He didn't have any right to stop me, so I hurdled anyway—and we both fell down. The other guys stopped running on account of the interference. A boy called Hubert Ackley the Third did it. He's a boy I never did used to like. Rich family, very good manners. Besides, the girl *I* like likes *him*. Helen Eliot. The more she likes him the more I get burned up and like her. I don't suppose she *notices* me, even. Well, I guess she can't very well *not* notice me, but I guess she thinks I think I'm a smart-aleck. I don't think she likes me at all. Maybe she *hates* me—the girl I love more than anybody else in the whole world—outside of my own family. You see, Mr. Grogan, this coach out there—his name is Byfield— well, I guess he's all right if you can understand him, only I don't know anybody who *can* understand him. He's always going around making trouble. Miss Hicks says he tells lies, too. Miss Hicks is our ancient-history teacher. She's been teaching at Ithaca

A Better World, a Better People

High School for thirty-five years. She taught my brother Marcus and my sister Bess. Of course, after we fell I got right up and began to run again and the other guys started too—fair and square. I knew something was wrong with my leg but I didn't stop to think about it at the time because I wanted to win. I didn't want to win just to win—I didn't want to beat Ackley—that guy surprised me. He stopped the others from running because Mr. Byfield had interfered with my running. Ackley's a good guy, I guess—he's just got refined manners, that's all. To tell you the truth, Mr. Grogan, the main reason I wanted to run the two-twenty low hurdles at first was because *Mr. Spangler* ran that race when he went to Ithaca High, but after what happened I wanted to win the race for Miss Hicks.

"You see, me and Ackley got into a little argument in the classroom, so of course she had to keep us in after school. Then this Byfield, the coach out there, came to Miss Hicks and lied to her. He took Ackley with him to run the race but he didn't take me. Miss Hicks said he lied the same as he used to lie when he was in her ancient history class. Her feelings were very hurt. I guess she just can't stand people going around that way telling lies. She talked to me—told me about my brother Marcus—and then she told me to go out and run the race. Mr. Spangler was Valley Champion of that race, and I guess I'd like to be Valley Champion some day myself, too. I don't think I'll be able to make it this year, though."

The messenger flexed his leg a couple of times. "I guess I'll rub some liniment on it tonight. Is the limp noticeable?"

"Well," Mr. Grogan said, "it's not *too* noticeable, but it is a *little* noticeable. Can you ride your bike all right?"

"Sure," Homer said. "It hurts a little, especially when I get the left leg up, so I try to do all the pumping with my right leg and let the left leg just sort of coast along. Sometimes I take it off the pedal and let it hang. That way it rests. I guess something's happened to the ligament—I'll rub it with liniment."

There was a pause. Then the old telegraph operator said, "You've changed some since you came to work three days ago, haven't you?"

"Have you noticed it, Mr. Grogan?" the messenger said. "Yeah, I guess I've changed all right. I guess I've grown up. And I guess it was *time* for me to grow up. I didn't know *anything* until I got this job. Oh, I knew a lot of things, but I didn't know the half of it, and I guess I never will, either. I guess nobody ever will. If anybody *should* know, though, I should. Everybody says I'm the smartest guy at Ithaca High, even people who don't like me. But I'm not so smart. I guess I'm just as backward as anybody in a lot of things—important things, too. I *want* to know and I'll *always* want to know. I'll always keep trying, but how can you ever know? How can any man ever really get it all straight so that it comes out even and makes sense?"

"Well," the old telegraph operator said, "I don't know *how* anybody is ever going to know, but I'm glad you've made up your mind to keep trying."

"I've *got* to keep trying," the messenger said. "You know, Mr. Grogan, I don't know about other people, and I don't know whether I can tell you this or not, but I'm not just the guy people *see*, I'm somebody else besides—somebody better. Sometimes *I* don't even know what to make of it." The messenger went on, because he was tired and something was wrong with his leg and he had taken the message of death into the happy home and because he knew the old telegraph operator was a good man. "The ideas I get," he said. "A different world, a better world, a better people, a better way of doing things." He paused a moment and then went on. "I'd be ashamed to say this to anybody but you, Mr. Grogan, but some day I'm going to go to work and do something. I don't know what it's going to be, but it's going to be *something*. I didn't used to know anything—I guess I was in a kind of happy daydream all the time. My whole family is happy. We're a happy kind of people, but I know I didn't used to know anything. Now I'm beginning to learn—just a little. Just a little more every day. This and that, and this and that and the other thing." The messenger stopped again, testing his leg to see if it had become healed as he talked. It hadn't. "I don't like the way things are, Mr. Grogan," he said. "I don't know why, but I want them to be better. I guess it's because I think they *ought* to be better. I've learned this much so far—that I don't know anything, but from now on I'm going to try to learn—all the time. I'm going to be watching all the time. I'm going to be thinking about it all the time. It makes a guy feel lonely, but I don't care about that. We're a happy people all right, but we're tough, too. I don't care about being lonely myself. I care about people who *aren't* tough being lonely and hurt, and it seems to me the world is full of people like that. I didn't know that before. Now I don't even care if Helen Eliot doesn't like me. I wish she did, though, but if she doesn't, that's O.K. I like *her*. I love her with all my heart, but if she wants to like Hubert Ackley the Third instead of me, that's O.K. He's a good guy, and I guess a refined girl like Helen Eliot likes to have a guy who's got good manners like Hubert Ackley the Third. I guess I haven't got any manners at all. I just do what I think is right and what I've *got* to do. At school I say a lot of funny things, but I don't do it to make trouble for the teachers. I do it because I've got to. Everybody's so sad or mixed up, and everything's so slow or wrong that I've just got to say funny things once in a while. I guess we ought to have some fun out of being alive. I don't suppose I could be refined or polite on purpose even if I wanted to be. I couldn't be polite if I didn't mean it."

The messenger flexed his leg again and spoke of it now as if it weren't his own. "Something's the matter with it," he said. He glanced up at the clock. "Well, Mr. Grogan," he said, "it's five minutes after twelve. I guess I'll go home. I don't feel very sleepy tonight, though. Tomorrow's Saturday. Saturday used to be the best day of all for me. No more, though. I guess I'll come down to the office. Maybe I can help out." He lifted the lunch-box off the delivery desk. "Wouldn't you like a sandwich now, Mr. Grogan?" he said.

"Well," the old telegraph operator said, "come to think of it, boy, yes, I would. I'm hungry now." Mr. Grogan took a sandwich out of the open box and bit into it. "Please thank your mother for me."

"Ah, it's nothing," the messenger said.

"No," Mr. Grogan said. "It *is* something. Please thank her for me."

"Yes, sir," Homer said, and left the office to go home.

CHAPTER 22

LET THERE BE LIGHT

Alone in the telegraph office, Mr. William Grogan, once young, once the fastest telegraph operator in the world, slowly began to clear off the work table. He hummed softly to himself a theme which had stayed in his memory from the earliest days of his life. As the old man did his work, Thomas Spangler, fresh from Corbett's and a little under the influence of alcohol and a mixture of giddy and solemn happiness, came into the office and went to his desk. He glanced over at the old telegraph operator, but did not speak. They had an understanding. Very often it was no matter at all to be at work for an hour or two without exchanging one word. Spangler lifted the good-luck egg off a pile of telegrams and studied its amazing symmetry. Then he put the egg back on the pile of telegrams and, remembering the girl pleasantly, he puckered up his lips in order to speak as she was given to speaking.

"You do love me, don't you?" he said. *"Yes, you do."*

The old telegraph operator glanced at the manager of the office.

"What's that, Tom?" he said.

"Willie," Spangler said, "what would you think of a young woman who tells you like this: *'You do love me, don't you? You do, you do! You know you do!'"*

"Well," Mr. Grogan said, "I don't know what I'd think."

"Would you like a young woman like that, Willie?" Spangler said, and then continued his imitation of the girl. *"You do love me, don't you?* That's what she says all the time."

Spangler rubbed his face as if to get over the great happiness and then said, "Anything doing tonight?"

"About the same," Mr. Grogan said, "except for the rain."

"How's the new messenger?" Spangler said. "Is he all right?"

"The best *I've* ever seen," the telegraph operator said. "What do *you* think of him?"

"I liked him from the time he came up and asked for a job," Spangler said. *"You do love me, don't you?"* He could not get over the wondrous way Diana Steed spoke the small words. "I'm glad you like the messenger," Spangler went on. "Don't bother to close the office, Willie. I'll do it myself. I've got a little work I want to attend to. That messenger has a kind of distinguished name, hasn't he? Homer Macauley. What do you think his father called him Homer for instead of Thomas or William or Henry or something like that?" Spangler didn't wait for a reply but went on to say, *"Yes, you do."*

Mr. Grogan said, "Homer's brother is called Ulysses, but his sister is called Bess."

"Homer, Ulysses, and Bess," Spangler said.

"And another brother," Mr. Grogan said, "is called Marcus. He's in the Army."

"Marcus, Homer, Ulysses and Bess," Spangler said. "Why don't you go home, Willie?"

"Home?" Mr. Grogan said. He smiled. "If you don't mind, Tom," he said, "I'd like to sit around with you. I've got nowhere to go and nothing to do after work except sleep, and I don't enjoy sleeping."

"Now, Willie," Spangler said as if he were speaking to a small boy, "I don't want you to worry. I know you *do* worry, but you don't need to. You're not old, and nobody in the world is going to put you on a pension. You know very well I'd be helpless in this office without you. You'll live to be a hundred, and you'll work every day of your life."

"Thanks," the old telegraph operator said. He paused and then said softly, "I had another little attack tonight. Oh, nothing serious. I felt it coming on for some time. The boy was here. I sent him for the medicine. I'm not supposed to take it, you know. I'm supposed to see the doctor and I'm supposed to rest."

"Doctors don't know everything, Willie," Spangler said. "They understand matter, not spirit, and you and I live in the spirit." And then suddenly he said, *"You do love me, don't you?* Doctors don't understand anything except matter," he said. "But maybe you ought to rest a little anyway."

"Oh, I'll rest," Mr. Grogan said. "I'll take the great rest, Tom."

"Willie," Spangler said, "go to Corbett's on the corner and have yourself a drink. Listen to the pianola. Come back and we'll talk over the old times—Wolinsky and Tomlinson and old man Davenport. Harry Bull the lineman, crazy Fred McIntyre, and wonderful Jerry Beattie. Go ahead now, Willie. Have yourself a drink or two, and when you come back we'll kick around the old times."

"I'm not supposed to drink, Tom," Mr. Grogan said. "You know I'm not supposed to drink."

"Sure I know you're not *supposed* to drink," Spangler said, "but I also know you *like* to drink and what a man likes to do is sometimes more important than what he is supposed to do—so go ahead and have yourself a drink."

"All right, Tom," Mr. Grogan said, and left the office.

On the sidewalk for the past three or four minutes a young man had passed the office several times, looking in. He came in at last and stood at the counter. Spangler noticed him and went over.

"How are you?" Spangler said, remembering the boy. "I thought you'd be on your way home to Pennsylvania long ago. Your mother sent you the money. You didn't need to come back to pay me."

"I didn't come back to pay you," the young man said. "I came back to get more, and I didn't come to beg it." He coughed. "I came to *take* it."

"What's the matter with you?" Spangler said.

"This is what's the matter with me," the young man said. From his right-hand coat pocket he brought out a revolver and held it in a trembling hand. Thomas Spangler, still a little drunk and happy, couldn't understand.

"Come on," the young man said. "Give me the money—all the money you've got in this place. Everybody's killing everybody and I don't mind if I kill you. And I don't mind if *I'm* killed. I'm excited and I don't want any trouble, but if you don't give me all the money—*now*—I'll shoot. Give me the money, and hurry."

Spangler drew open the cash drawer and took the money out of the several compartments. He placed

the money—currency, rolls of coin and open coins—
on the counter before the boy.

"I'd give you the money, anyway," he said, "but
not because you're pointing a gun at me. I'd give
it to you because you need it. Here. This is all the
money there is. Take it and get on a train and go
home. Go back where you belong. I won't report a
theft. I'll make it good myself. There's about seventy-five dollars here."

He waited for the boy to take the money, but the
boy wouldn't touch it.

"I mean it," Spangler said. "Take the money
and go—you need it. You're no criminal, and you're
not so sick you can't get well. Your mother's waiting
for you. This money is a gift from me to her. You
won't be a thief taking it. Just take the money, put
that gun away and go home. *Throw* the gun away—
you'll feel better."

The young man put the gun back into his coat
pocket. Over his trembling mouth he placed the
hand which had held the gun. "I ought to go out
and shoot myself," he said.

"Don't talk like a fool," the manager of the
telegraph office said. He gathered the money together and held it out to the young man. "Now
here," he said. "This is all the money there is. Take
it and go home, that's all. If you like, leave the
gun here with me. Here's your money. Yes, *yours*--
it *is* yours, if you've got to take a gun out to get it!
I know how you feel because I've felt the same way.

We've all felt the same way. The graveyards and penitentiaries are full of good American kids who've had bad luck and hard times. They're not criminals. Here," he said gently, "take this money. Go home."

The young man brought the gun out of his pocket and pushed it across the counter to Spangler, who dropped it into the cash drawer.

"I don't know who you are," he said, "but no one has ever talked to me the way you have. I don't want the gun, and I won't take the money, and I *am* going home. I bummed my way out here, and I'll bum my way back." He coughed a moment and then said, "I don't know where my mother got the thirty dollars. I know she has no money to spare. I spent some of the money drinking. I gambled some, and—"

"Come on in and sit down," Spangler said. After a moment the young man went to the chair beside Spangler's desk. Spangler sat down on the desk. "What's the matter?" he said to the young man.

"I don't know exactly," the young man said. "I think I'm sick—maybe T.B. I'm not sure. If I haven't got it, I guess I *ought* to have it, the way I've been living. I don't like to complain. I've had a lot of bad luck, but I know it's my own fault. I'll go now. Thanks a lot—I'll try to remember you some day." The young man turned to leave the office

"Wait a minute," Spangler said. "Sit down. Take it easy. You've got a lot of time—*now*. You're not rushing things any more. From now on, move a little slower. What's a fellow like you interested in?"

"I don't know," the young man said. "I don't know which way to go, or what to do when I get there, or what to believe, or anything. My father was a preacher, but he's been dead since I was three years old. I just don't know what to do." He looked at Spangler. "What *is* there to do?" he said.

"Oh, nothing in particular," Spangler said. "Anything. It doesn't matter what a man does. Any good honest work."

"I've always been restless and dissatisfied," the young man said. "I don't know what it is. Nothing means anything to me. I don't like people. I don't like being near them. I don't trust them. I don't like the way they live or talk or the things they believe, or the way they push each other around."

"Every man in the world feels that way at one time or another," Spangler said.

"It's not that I don't understand *myself*," the young man said. "I guess I do. I've got no alibis. I'm responsible for everything. Now, I'm just tired and fed-up and sick. Nothing interests me. The whole world's gone crazy. I can't live the kind of life I want to live and I don't feel like living any other kind. It's not money that I want or need. I know I could get a job, especially now. But I don't like the people you've got to get jobs from. They're no good. I don't like being humble to them, and I can't let anybody push me around. I tried to hold a few jobs in York, Pennsylvania. I always had a fight and got fired. Three or four days, a week, or a week and a half. The longest I ever held a job was one month.

"I tried to enlist in the Army in York because I thought that might be a good thing to do—go somewhere—get killed maybe. If they boss you in the Army at least it's for something that's supposed to be halfway decent. I don't know whether it really *is* decent or not, but at least it's supposed to be. They turned me down. I couldn't pass the physical examination. It wasn't my lungs only—it was other things too. I didn't bother to find out." The young man began to cough again, but this time he coughed for almost a full minute. Spangler brought a small bottle out of the desk drawer.

"Here," he said, "take a drink of this."

"Thanks," the young man said. "I drink a little too much, but I *need* a drink now." He took a swallow from the bottle, then handed it back to Spangler. "Thanks," he said.

Spangler decided he ought to urge the young man to go on talking. "What do you read?" he said.

"Oh, everything," the young man said. "At least I used to when I was home. My father had a lot of books—not religious books only—good books—by good writers. My favorite was William Blake. Maybe you know his stuff. Shakespeare, Milton, Pope, Donne, Dickens, Thackeray—all of them. I read every book my father had—some of them twice, a few three times. I used to like to read, but no more. Now I don't even want to look at newspapers. I *know* the news. The news is corruption and murder all over the place, every day, and not one man in the world shocked about it." He held his head in his hands and, speaking softly, he went on without looking up. "I can't thank you for what you've done and for the kind of human being you are," he said. "I must tell you I would have shot you if you had been afraid of me or unkind. Everybody in the world is afraid or unkind. I know now that I didn't come here with a gun for *money*. I don't know whether you will understand, but I came here with a gun to find out once and for all if the only man in the world I have ever known who has been decent to another man just to be decent—just for itself—was *truly* so. I came to find out if it wasn't an accident. I couldn't believe anybody could be really decent, because it made my whole feeling about everything and everybody untrue—the feeling I have had for a long time that the human race is hopeless and corrupt, that there isn't one man in the world worthy of being truly human, worthy of another man's respect. For a long time I've had contempt for the pathetic as well as for the proud, and then suddenly thousands of miles from home, in a strange city, I found a man who was decent. It bothered me. It bothered me for a long time. I couldn't believe it. I had to find out. I wanted it to be true. I wanted to believe it, because I've been telling myself for years: 'Let me find one man uncorrupted by the world so that *I* may be uncorrupted, so that I may believe and live.' I wasn't sure the first time we met, but I'm sure now. I want nothing more from you. You've given me everything I want. You can't give me anything more. You understand, I know. When I get up it shall be to say good-by. You needn't worry about me. I'm going home where I belong. I'm not going to die of this sickness. I'm going to live. And now I'm going to know *how* to live." The young man did not lift his head for a moment. Then he got up slowly and looked at Spangler. "Thanks a lot," he said.

Spangler watched the young man walk out of the office. He went to the cash drawer and put the money back where it belonged. He took the young man's revolver and unloaded it. He put the revolver back in the drawer and dropped the shells into his coat pocket. Then he went to the steel rack where each day's telegrams were tied into a bundle. In one bundle he found the telegram the boy had sent his mother. The manager of the telegraph office took a fresh telegraph blank and began to write a telegram. He wrote:

MRS. MARGARET STRICKMAN
1874 BIDDLE STREET
YORK, PENNSYLVANIA

DEAR MA: THANKS FOR THE MONEY. WILL BE HOME SOON. EVERYTHING FINE.

He read the words of the message and then decided to change "fine" to "O.K." Then he remembered

the young man a moment and added, "Love, John."
He went to Mr. Grogan's place at the telegraph table
and called for an operator. His call was answered
after several moments and then Spangler tapped out
the telegram, after which he talked to the operator
at the other end, smiling as he listened to the dots
and dashes and made his answers. When he was
through talking he got up and went to his own desk.

William Grogan came in and sat in the chair
where the young man had been sitting.

"How do you feel now?" Spangler said to the old
telegraph operator.

"Better, of course," Mr. Grogan said. "I had *two*
drinks, Tom. I listened to the soldiers singing. They
love that pianola and those old songs—songs they
never heard before."

"*You do love me, don't you?*" Spangler said. "*Yes,
you do. You know you do.* That's what she says,
Willie," Spangler said to the old telegraph operator,
"and that's the way she says it. I believe I'm going to
marry her."

Spangler stopped dreaming of Diana Steed a moment to study the face of his old friend. "The old
songs," he said, "are O.K."

"Tom," Mr. Grogan said, "remember the way old
Davenport used to sing those ballads?"

"Sure," Spangler said, "as long as this office is here
I'll hear him. I can hear him now. But not old ballads only—church songs, too. Don't forget the church

songs old Davenport used to sing every Sunday."

"I haven't forgotten them," Mr. Grogan said. "I remember every one of them. Of course he liked to pretend he was an unbeliever, but all day Sunday he sang hymns—chewing tobacco, sending telegrams, singing, and squirting tobacco juice out of his mouth into the spittoon. First thing in the morning he'd start out with 'Welcome, delightful morn, thou day of sacred rest.' He was a great man, Tom. Then he'd holler out, 'This is the day of light. Let there be light today.' "

"I remember," Spangler said, "I remember. *Let there be light today.* And then he'd spit tobacco juice into the cuspidor."

"Then," Mr. Grogan said, "he would sing, 'Lord, God of morning and of night, We thank Thee for Thy gift of light.' The great unbeliever—and more than anything he loved light and life. And then at the end of the day he would get up from his chair slowly, stretch himself and sing very softly, 'Now the day is over, night is drawing nigh.' He knew all of the good old songs, and he loved every one of them. 'Saviour,' he would shout, pretending to be an unbeliever who was mocking, 'Saviour, breathe an evening blessing, Ere repose our spirits seal; Sin and want we come confessing, Thou canst save and Thou canst heal.' "

The telegraph operator became silent to remember his friend who had been dead these long, long years. "It's the truth, Tom," he said. "It's the truth."

The manager of the telegraph office smiled at his old friend and patted him on the shoulder as he moved to turn off the lights and close the office for the night.

CHAPTER 23

DEATH, DON'T GO TO ITHACA!

Homer Macauley was in bed at last, tossing and turning. He dreamed he was running the two-twenty low hurdles again, but every time he got to a hurdle, Byfield was there to stop him. He hurdled anyway and they went down. At every hurdle Byfield was there. Finally the injury to Homer's leg was so painful that when he tried to run, he fell. He got up and pasted Byfield in the mouth. He shouted out to the man, "Byfield, you can't stop me! You can never stop me—low hurdles, high hurdles, any kind of hurdles!"

Death, Don't Go to Ithaca!

He began to run again, limping at first but soon running well, but the next hurdle was inhumanly high—eight feet—nevertheless, Homer Macauley, perhaps the greatest man in Ithaca, California, went over the hurdle with perfect form.

Next in the dream he was in his uniform riding his bicycle swiftly down a narrow street. Suddenly Byfield stood in the way. But Homer pushed toward the man more swiftly than ever. "Byfield," he shouted, "I told you—you can't stop me!" He lifted upward on the handlebars of his bicycle, and the bicycle began to rise and fly. It flew directly over Byfield's head and came down lightly on the other side of him. But just as it reached the pavement, Byfield stood in the way again! Again the bicycle left the street and began to fly over the man. But this time it stayed aloft, suspended twenty feet over Byfield's head. The man stood in the street, amazed and displeased. "You can't do that!" he shouted at the messenger. "You're breaking the law of gravity."

"What do I care about the law of gravity?" Homer shouted down at the man in the street, "or the law of averages, or the law of supply and demand, or any other law? *You can't stop me!* You can't stop me, that's all! Worm, rust and rot—I have no time for you." The messenger rode on through space, leaving the ugly man alone in the street, as inferior as any inferiority could ever be.

Now Homer flew high on his bicycle, among dark

clouds. As the messenger rode through the sky, he watched another bicycle rider in a messenger's uniform very much like his own but moving even faster than himself, push out of black cloud. The second messenger, strangely, seemed to be Homer himself, but at the same time he seemed to be someone Homer feared. Therefore Homer raced after the second messenger to find out who he really was.

The two riders raced a good long distance before Homer began to catch up. Suddenly the other messenger turned to look at Homer, and Homer was amazed that the messenger looked exactly like himself, but at the same time was unmistakably—not so much in appearance as in feeling—the messenger of Death. The riders were swiftly coming to Ithaca. Homer raced after the messenger of Death, moving swifter than ever before. Far down in the distance he could see the lonely lights of the town and the beautiful lonely streets and houses. Homer was determined to head off the other messenger, to keep him away from Ithaca. Nothing in the whole world was more important than to keep this messenger from reaching Ithaca.

The two riders raced hard and decently, with no tricks of any kind. They were both tiring now, but at last Homer was alongside the other rider, and was heading him away from Ithaca. Then, with a sudden burst of speed, the other messenger drew away and turned back toward the little town. Deeply disappointed in himself but still racing with all his might, Homer watched the other messenger ride on toward Ithaca, leaving Homer far behind. Now Homer could race no longer. There was no energy left with which to chase the messenger of Death. The boy almost collapsed on his bicycle, sobbing bitterly. The bicycle began to fall, and Homer began to cry out to the other messenger, "Come back! Don't go to Ithaca! Leave them alone! Come back!"

The boy sobbed with terrible grief.

In the house on Santa Clara Avenue the dreamer's little brother Ulysses stood beside Homer and listened to him. He went through the dark house to his mother's bed and shook her. When she sat up, he took her hand and without a word they went together to Homer's bed. Mrs. Macauley listened to her son a moment, then put Ulysses back in his bed, tucked him in, and sat down beside the weeping boy. She spoke to him very softly.

"Be still now, Homer," she said. "Rest now. You are very tired. You must rest. Sleep now. Sleep peacefully." The messenger began to stop sobbing and soon his troubled expression went away. "Sleep now," his mother said to him. "Sleep peacefully."

The boy began to sleep. The mother looked over at her youngest son and he, too, was now asleep. In the corner of the room she saw Matthew Macauley standing, watching, smiling. She got up quietly, took the alarm clock, and went back to her own room.

The Human Comedy

The messenger's sleep moved from the realm of terror to one of warmth and light and comfort. Homer Macauley, in this new sleep, found himself lying on his back under a fig tree beside a brook. "This," he said to himself in his sleep, "would be up by Riverdale where I saw the fig tree by the little stream, with the sun burning with a kind of laughter that made everything else laugh. I remember this place. It was last summer and Marcus and I came here to swim and then we sat on the bank of the stream and talked about what we would do in the world." And now, knowing the pleasantness of the place he had reached and feeling the warmth of his memory of it, he stretched out comfortably on the grass under the tree—and forgot completely that he was asleep.

He was in the same old clothes he wore that summer day with Marcus. Before him, stuck into the soft earth, he saw the fishing pole, but this was not from that summer day—it was from a long, long time ago. Now, far away through the wilderness of grass and bough Homer Macauley beheld the wondrous Helen Eliot, barefoot like himself, and in a plain gingham dress, walking over a narrow path toward him. "That's Helen Eliot," Homer said to himself. "That's the girl I love." He sat up smiling, watched her walk, and then got to his feet and went to greet her. Without a word and with something like solemnity, Homer took the girl's hand and together they walked to the tree. There he swiftly dived into the little stream. Homer watched the girl come to the edge of the stream, stand a moment, and then dive. Still solemn, they swam around in the little stream and after a while they left it together.

CHAPTER 24

THE APRICOT TREE

Ulysses Macauley was up very early, skipping
through the morning's first sunlight toward the yard
of a man who owned a cow. When he reached the
yard, Ulysses saw the cow. The small boy stood and
watched the cow a long time. At last the man who
owned the cow came out of the small house. He
was carrying a bucket and a stool. The man went
straight to the cow and began to milk. Ulysses
moved in closer until finally he was directly behind the man. Still, he couldn't see enough, so he
knelt down, almost under the cow. The man saw
the boy but did not say anything. He went right on

milking. The cow, however, turned and looked at Ulysses. Ulysses looked back at the cow. It seemed that the cow did not like to have the boy so close. Ulysses got out from under the cow, walked away, and watched from near by. The cow, in turn, watched Ulysses, so that the small boy believed they were friends.

On his way home, Ulysses stopped to watch a man who was building a barn. The man was high-strung, nervous, impatient, and should never have undertaken the work. He labored furiously, making all kinds of mistakes, while Ulysses watched and did not understand.

Ulysses got back to Santa Clara Avenue just in time to see Mr. Arena go off to work on his bicycle. Mary Arena waved to him from the porch and then went back into the house.

It was Saturday morning in Ithaca, the school boys' happiest day. Out of a house not far away came a boy of eight or nine. Ulysses waved to him and the boy waved back. This boy was Lionel Cabot, the neighborhood half-wit, but all the same a great human being, faithful, generous and sweet-tempered. After a moment Lionel looked over at Ulysses again, and, for want of something better to do, waved again. Ulysses waved back. This continued at frequent intervals until August Gottlieb came out of his house next door to Ara's Market.

Auggie had been the leader of the neighborhood boys since Homer Macauley had retired from that position at the age of twelve. The new leader looked around for his followers. He rejected Lionel as too dumb and Ulysses as too little, but waved a greeting to each of them nevertheless. He then went out to the middle of the street and whistled, newsboy style. It was a loud whistle, very authoritative, very commanding, and absolutely final. Auggie waited with the confidence of a man who knows what he is doing and what results he is going to get. Immediately windows were opened and replies were whistled. Soon a number of boys came running to the corner. In less than three minutes the gang was together—Auggie Gottlieb, the leader, Nickie Paloota, Alf Rife, and Shag Manoogian.

"Where are we going, Auggie?" Nickie said.

"To see if Henderson's apricots are ripe," Auggie said.

"Can I come, Auggie?" Lionel said.

"O.K., Lionel," Auggie said. "If they're ripe, will you steal some?"

"It's a sin to steal," Lionel said.

"Not apricots," Auggie said, making an important distinction. "Ulysses," he said, "you go home. This is not for little boys. It's dangerous."

Ulysses moved away three steps, stopped and watched. He wasn't hurt or offended by Auggie's orders. He understood the code. He was just not old enough yet, that's all. But while he respected the law, he couldn't resist wanting to be in the gang anyhow.

The Apricot Tree

The boys started off for Henderson's. Instead of going by way of streets and sidewalks, they took alleys, crossed empty lots, and climbed over fences. They wanted to get there the hard way, the adventurous way. Not far behind, at a safe distance, Ulysses followed.

"Ripe apricots are just about the best-tasting fruit in the world," Auggie said to the members of his gang.

"Do apricots get ripe in March?" Nickie Paloota said.

"It's almost April," Auggie said. *"Early* apricots get ripe in no time if the sun shines a lot."

"It's been raining lately, though," Alf Rife said.

"Where do you think apricots get their juice from?" Auggie said. "From water—from rain. Rain is just as important as sunshine to apricots."

"Sunshine in the daytime, rain at night," Shag Manoogian said. "Warm them up, give them water. I'll bet there's a lot of ripe apricots on the tree."

"Boy, I hope so," Alf Rife said.

"It's too early for apricots," Nickie Paloota said. "They weren't ripe last year until June."

"That was last year," Auggie said. "This is this year."

From a distance of about one hundred yards the boys stopped to admire the famous apricot tree—all green and pretty, very old and very big. It stood in the corner of Henderson's backyard. For ten years the boys of the neighborhood had raided old man Henderson's apricot tree. In the broken-down house every spring Mr. Henderson had watched their coming with fascination and delight—always satisfying the boys by appearing at the last minute and scaring them away. Now in the house at a curtained window Mr. Henderson looked up from his book.

"Well, look at that!" he said to himself. "Coming to steal apricots in March, in the dead of Winter. Look at them!" He peeked out at the boys again, whispering as if he were one of them. "Coming to get apricots off old man Henderson's tree," he said. "Here they come. Slowly, now. Ha-ha," he laughed, "look at them! And look at that little one! Surely not more than four years old. He's a new one. Come on, come on! Come to the wonderful old tree. If I could ripen the apricots for you to steal, I'd do it—"

Mr. Henderson watched the boys as Auggie instructed, directed and led the attack. The boys surrounded the tree cautiously, fearfully, and with a mingling in their hearts of hope and fear. Even if the apricots were green, they were on Henderson's tree and belonged to him, and therefore their coming for the apricots was the same as if the apricots were ripe—therefore they *hoped* the apricots *were* ripe. But they were afraid, too. They were afraid of Henderson, they were afraid of sin, of capture and guilt, and they were afraid they were a little too

168

early. They were afraid the apricots weren't ripe yet.

"Maybe he ain't home, Auggie," Nickie Paloota whispered as the boys almost reached the tree.

"He's home," Auggie said. "He's *always* home. He's hiding, that's all. It's a trap. He wants to catch us. Careful, everybody. There's no telling where he'll be. Ulysses, you go home."

Obediently Ulysses retreated three steps and stopped to watch the magnificent duel with the magnificent tree.

"Are they ripe, Auggie?" Shag said. "Do you see any color?"

"Only green," Auggie said. "That's leaves. The apricots are underneath. Easy now, everybody. Where's Lionel?"

"Here I am," Lionel whispered. He was terribly afraid.

"Well," Auggie said, "be on your toes. If you see old man Henderson, run!"

"Where is he?" Lionel said as if Henderson might be invisible or no bigger than a rabbit, something likely to jump up suddenly out of the grass.

"What do you mean where is he?" Auggie said. "He's in the house, I guess. But you can never tell about Henderson. He might be hiding outside some place, waiting to take us by surprise."

"Are *you* going to climb the tree, Auggie?" Alf Rife said.

"Who else?" Auggie said. "Sure I'm going to

climb the tree, but let's see if the apricots are ripe first."

"Ripe or green," Shag Manoogian said, "we want to steal at least *some* of them, Auggie."

"Don't worry," Auggie said. "We will. If they're ripe, we'll steal a *lot* of them."

"What are you going to say at Sunday School tomorrow, Auggie?" Lionel said.

"Stealing apricots isn't stealing, like stealing in the Bible, Lionel," Auggie said. "This is different."

"Then what are you scared of?" Lionel said.

"Who's scared?" Auggie said. "We've just got to be careful, that's all. What's the use getting caught if you can get away?"

"I don't see any ripe apricots," Lionel said.

"You see a tree, don't you?" Auggie said.

"I see a tree, all right," Lionel said. "That's *all,* though—just a big tree—all green. It sure is pretty, too, Auggie."

Now the gang was almost under the tree. Ulysses followed not far behind. He was absolutely unafraid. He didn't understand at all, but he was sure this was very important stuff—something about trees, something about apricots. The boys studied the branches of the old apricot tree, green with fine young leaf. The apricots were all very small, very green, and obviously very hard.

"Not ripe yet," Alf Rife said.

"Yeah," Auggie admitted. "I guess they need a couple days more. Maybe next Saturday."

'Next Saturday—*sure*," Shag said.

"There's a *lot* of them, though," Auggie said.

"We can't go back empty-handed, Auggie," Shag said. "We've got to get at least *one* of them—green or ripe—*one* of them anyway."

"O.K.," Auggie said. "I'll get it. Now the rest of you be ready to run." Auggie dashed to the tree, swung up into it on one of its lower branches while the gang and Mr. Henderson and Ulysses watched with fascination, amazement, and admiration. Then Mr. Henderson stepped out of the house onto the back-porch steps. All the boys went off like a school of startled minnows.

"Auggie!" Shag Manoogian shouted. *"Henderson!"*

Like a frightened orang-outang in the jungle, Auggie bounced around in the tree, hung from a branch, and then dropped to the ground. He was running almost before his feet touched the ground, but he noticed Ulysses and stopped suddenly, shouting at the boy, "Ulysses! Run—*run!*"

Ulysses, however, didn't budge. He couldn't figure it out. Auggie rushed back to the small boy, lifted him off his feet, and ran with him while Henderson watched. When all the boys had disappeared and everything was quiet again, the old man smiled and looked up into the tree. Then he turned around and went back into the house.

CHAPTER 25

BE HAPPY! BE HAPPY!

One by one the members of August Gottlieb's Secret Society returned from their escape from old man Henderson and gathered in front of Ara's Market to wait there for the arrival of their leader. At last this great man was observed by his devoted followers coming around the alley holding the hand of Ulysses Macauley. The members of the Society waited silently for the arrival of the leader, who was soon with them. The face of the leader was searched by each of the followers and then the one named Alf Rife said, "Did you get an apricot, Auggie?"

The leader looked at this faithless one and said, "You don't have to ask that. You saw me in the tree. You *know* I got an apricot."

Now all the members spoke in one voice. (All, that is, excepting Lionel, who was not really a member at all.) They said with great admiration, "Let's see it, Auggie. Let's look at the apricot."

The little boy Ulysses watched everything, still completely unsure of the mysterious values involved but still certain that whatever these values might be they were surely of greater importance than anything else in the world—at that moment at least.

"Let's see the apricot you stole, Auggie," the members of the Society said again. "Come on, let's see it."

August Gottlieb quietly fished into the pocket of his overalls and brought out a clenched fist which he thrust before him. His followers gathered around and looked directly upon the fist. When everyone was appropriately quiet and respectful, August Gottlieb opened his fist.

There in the palm of his hand was a small green apricot the size of a quail egg.

The followers of the great religious leader smiled at the miraculous object in the palm of his hand, and Lionel—the kindest of them all, even though he was not a bona-fide member of the religious sect —lifted Ulysses so that he too could see the small green object. Having seen the green apricot, Ulysses squirmed, got down, and then ran for home, not disappointed, only eager to tell someone.

Now, out of his store, stepped Ara himself, the man who had established Ara's Market in this neighborhood of Ithaca, California, seven years ago. He was a tall, lean-faced, melancholy and yet comical man in a white grocer's apron. He stood a moment on the small porch of the store to look down at the new Messiah and his disciples and to listen to their delighted expressions of adoration.

"Auggie, you!" he said. "You, Shag! Nickie! Alfo, you! Lionel, you!—what you call this? United States Congress Washington? Go some odder place hold important meeting. This market, not Congress."

"Oh, sure, Mr. Ara," August Gottlieb said. "We'll go across the street to the empty lot. Do you want to see an apricot?"

"You got apricot?" the grocer said. "Where you get apricot?"

"Off a tree," Auggie said. "Want to see it?"

"Is not apricot now," the grocer said. "Apricot come in two more month. In Maytime."

"This is a March apricot," August Gottlieb, the leader of the whirling-dervishes, said to the grocer. "Here," he said, "look at it." Again he opened his fist, revealing the small hard green object. "Look at it, Mr. Ara," Auggie said, and then paused. "Pretty?"

"All right, all right," Mr. Ara said. "Pretty. Very

fine apricot. Now go hold meeting United States Congress Washington some odder place. Today Saturday. Market open for business. Don't crowd small store first thing in morning. Give chance. Small store get scared, run away."

"O.K., Mr. Ara," Auggie said, "we won't crowd your store. We'll go across the street now. Come on, you guys."

Mr. Ara studied the small migration of the religious fanatics. He was about to go back into the store when a small boy who resembled him came out of the store and stood beside him.

"Papa?" the small boy said.

"Hah, John?" the father said to his son, speaking in their own language.

"Give me apple," the son said to the father. He spoke earnestly, almost sadly.

The father took the son by the hand and together they went into the store to the counter where the fresh fruit was stacked in piles.

"Apple?" the father said to the boy. He took an apple from the pile—the very best apple in the pile—and handed it to the boy. "All right," he said—"apple."

The father went behind the counter of his store to wait for a customer, and in the meantime to look upon his son, surely as melancholy as himself, even though there was a difference of at least forty years in their ages. The son took one enormous bite of the apple, chewed it slowly, swallowed it, and then

for a moment seemed to think about it, while the
father himself thought about it too. The apple did
not make the boy happy. He put it down on the
counter in front of his father and then looked up at
the man. There they were, in Ithaca, California,
probably seven thousand miles from what had been
for centuries their home in the world. Naturally
there was a loneliness in each of them, but no one
could know for sure that the same loneliness might
not be in them had they been seven thousand miles
away, back home. There on the floor of his store
stood the father's son, and the father looked at the
son—at his own face in the boy, his own eyes, and
beyond the eyes surely his own unhappiness. There
was the same man, only younger. The father took
the rejected apple, attacked it with an enormous
bite, making a crackling sound, and stood chewing
and swallowing. He might have been bitter from the
swiftness and noisiness of his chewing. An apple was
too good a thing in the world to be wasted, and
therefore if his son would not eat it, then he must
eat it, even though he had no passion for apples or
for their flavor. He simply knew that it was wrong
to waste anything. He continued to bite into the
apple, to chew, and to swallow. At last, however, it
was a little too much—there was a little too much
apple. It would be necessary to waste *some* of it.
With recklessness and perhaps a small amount of
regret, he threw the remains of the apple into the
garbage can.

Be Happy! Be Happy!

Now the son spoke again. "Papa?" he said.

"Hah, John?" the father said.

"Give me orange," the boy said.

The father selected the biggest orange in the neat pile of oranges and handed it to the boy. "Orange?" he said. "All right—orange."

The boy bit into the peel of the orange, then began to finish the job of peeling with his fingers, working slowly but efficiently at first but after a moment accelerating his effort with such an intensity that even the father began to feel, as surely the son felt, that beneath the peeling of this growth of tree would be not simply an orange but the heart's final happiness. The boy placed the peelings of the orange on the counter in front of his father, broke the orange in half, peeled off one section, put it in his mouth, chewed, and swallowed. But alas, no. It was truly an orange, but it was truly *not* the heart's final happiness. The son waited a moment, then put the rest of the orange in front of his father. Again the father took up the unfinished work and silently began trying to finish it. But soon the limit was reached, and a little less than half of the orange went into the garbage can.

"Papa?" the boy said after a moment, and again the father replied, "Hah, John?"

"Give me candy," the boy said.

"Candy?" the father said. "All right—candy." From the candy showcase the father selected the most popular five-cent bar of candy and handed it to the boy. The boy studied this manufactured substance, removed the wax paper, took a big bite out of the chocolate-covered candy and again slowly chewed and swallowed. But again it was nothing—only candy—sweet, yes; otherwise, nothing, nothing. Once again the son returned to the father another substance of the world which had failed to bring him happiness. Patiently the father accepted the responsibility—to avoid waste. He picked up the candy bar, started to bite into it and then changed his mind. He turned and threw the candy into the garbage can. For some reason he felt bitterly angry, and in his heart he cursed some people seven thousand miles away who had once seemed to him to be inhuman, or at least ignorant. *Those dogs!* he said in his heart.

Once again the boy spoke to his father.

"Papa?" he said.

"Hah, John?" the father said.

"Give me banana," the boy said.

The father sighed this time but did not abandon all faith. "Banana?" he said. "All right—banana." He examined the bunch of bananas hanging over the piles of fruit and finally discovered what he believed to be the very best—the ripest and the sweetest banana of the bunch. He plucked this banana off the bunch and handed it to the boy.

At last a customer came into the store. The customer was a man Mr. Ara had never seen before—a stranger. The storekeeper and the customer nodded slightly to one another in greeting, and then the man said, "You got cookies?"

"Cook-ies?" the grocer said eagerly. "What kind cook-ies you want?"

Another customer came into the store. This customer was Ulysses Macauley. He stood to one side, listening and watching, waiting his turn.

"You got cookies, raisins in?" the man said to the grocer.

"Cook-ies, raisins in?" the grocer said. This was a problem. "Cook-ies, raisins in," the grocer said again, almost whispering. "Cook-ies, raisins in," he said still again. The grocer looked around the store. The grocer's son put the banana on the counter in front of his father—rejected.

"Papa?" the boy said.

The father looked at the boy and then spoke very swiftly. "You want apple," he said. "I give you apple. You want orange. I give you orange. You want candy. I give you candy. You want banana. I give you banana. What you want *now?*"

"Cookies," the boy said.

"What kind cook-ies you want?" the father said to the boy, not forgetting the customer, and in fact, speaking *to* the customer, but at the same time speaking to his son, and at the same time speaking to everybody—everybody, everywhere—everybody wanting things.

"Cookies, raisins in," the boy said.

With furious restraint the father almost whispered

his reply to his son, but instead of looking at his son he looked at the customer. "I got no cook-ies," he whispered. *"No* kind cook-ies. What you want cook-ies? I got everything, but no cook-ies. What's cook-ies? What you want?"

"Cookies," the man said patiently, "for small boy."

"I got no cook-ies," the grocer said again. "I got small boy too." The grocer pointed to his own son. "I give him apple, orange, candy, banana, lots of good things." He looked the customer straight in the eye, and almost as if he were angry, he said, "What you want?"

"My broder's boy," the customer said. "He's got influenza. He cry—he want cookies. 'Cookies, raisins in,' he say."

But every man lives his own life and every life has its own theme, so that again the grocer's son looked at his father and said, "Papa?"

But now the father refused to look at the boy. Instead he looked at the man whose nephew was ill and wanted cookies with raisins in them. He looked at the man with understanding, with sympathy, and yet with a kind of peasant rage, not against the man but against the world itself, against disease, against pain, against loneliness, against the heart wanting what it can never have. The grocer was angry at himself too because even though he had established this market in Ithaca, California, seven thousand miles from home, he did not have cookies with raisins in them, he did not have that which the sick boy wanted. The grocer pointed at his son and spoke to the man.

"Apple," the grocer said, "orange, candy, banana —no cookies. He's my boy. Three year old. Not sick. He want many things. He want apple. He want orange. He want candy. He want banana. I don't know what he want. Nobody know what he want. He just want. He look at God. He say, Give me dis, give me dat—but he never satisfied. Always he want. Always he's feel bad. Poor God has got nothing for sadness. He give everything — world — sunshine — moder — fader — broder — sister — onkle — cousin — house, farm, stove, table, bed—poor God give everything—but nobody happy—everybody like small boy sick with influenza—everybody say give me cookies— raisins in." The grocer stopped a moment to take a very deep breath. When he exhaled he said very loudly to the customer, *"Is no cookies—raisins in."*

The grocer began to move with an impatience and a fury which were almost majestic. First he took a paper bag and snapped it open. Then he began to toss things into the bag. "Here's orange," he said, "very pretty. Here's apple. Wonderful. Here's banana. Taste very good." Now, gently, and with great courtesy and sincere sympathy for the man and for the man's sick nephew, the grocer handed the bag to the customer. "Take to little boy," he said. "Maybe he not cry. Here, take good things to little boy.

Don't pay. I no want money." And then again he said very softly, "Is no cookies, raisins in."

"He cry," the man said. "He feel very bad. He say, 'Cookies, raisins in.' Thank you very much, but we give small boy apple, orange, odder things." The man put the bag down on the counter. "Sick boy say," he said to the grocer, " 'Give me cookies, raisins in.' Apple, orange—no good. Cookies. Excuse me," the man said. "I go try chain store. Maybe *they* got cookies, raisins in."

"All right, my friend," the grocer whispered. "All right. You go try chain store—but they no got cookies, raisins in. Nobody got."

Almost shyly the stranger left the store. For a full minute the grocer stood behind the counter of his store staring at his son. Suddenly he began to speak in his own language, Armenian.

"The world's gone mad," he said to the small boy. "In Russia alone, so near our own country, our own beautiful little nation, millions of people, millions of children, every day go hungry. They are cold, pathetic, barefooted— They walk around—no place to sleep—they pray for a piece of dry bread—somewhere to lie down and rest—one night of peaceful sleep. And what about us? What do we do? Here in Ithaca, California, in this great country, America. What do we do? We wear good clothes. We put on good shoes every morning when we get up from sleep. We walk around with no one in the streets to come with guns or to burn our houses or to murder our children or brothers or fathers. We take rides out into the beautiful country in automobiles. We eat the best food. Every night when we go to bed we sleep—and then what are we? We are discontented. We are *still* discontented." The grocer shouted this amazing truth at his little son with terrible love for the boy. "Apple," he said, "orange, candy, banana, for God's sake, little fellow, don't do this! If I do it, you are my son, better than me, and therefore you must not do this. Be happy! Be happy! I am unhappy, but *you* must be happy." He pointed to the back door of the store which led into the house, and obediently, very sober-faced, the little boy left the store and entered the house.

Now the grocer spent a moment trying to compose himself. At last he believed he was calm enough to speak quietly to the customer in the store, Ulysses Macauley. He turned to the boy and tried to be cheerful. He even smiled. "What you want, little boy Ulysses?" he said.

"Mush," Ulysses said.

"What kind mush you want?" the grocer said.

"H-O," Ulysses said.

"Two kinds H-O, little boy Ulysses," the grocer said—"regular kind, quick-cooking kind. Two kinds. Slow, quick. Old, new. What kind your mama want, little boy Ulysses?"

Ulysses thought about this a moment and then said, "H-O."

"Old kind or new kind?" the grocer said.

But the little boy didn't know, so the grocer decided for him. "All right," he said, "new kind, modern. Eighteen cents, please, little boy Ulysses."

Ulysses opened his fist and thrust his arm out toward the grocer, who took the quarter from the boy's hand. The grocer handed Ulysses the change, saying, "Eighteen cents, nineteen, twenty, and nickel —twenty-five. Thank you, little boy Ulysses."

"Yes, sir," Ulysses said. He took the package of oatmeal and walked out of the store. It was very difficult to understand anything. First it was apricots on a tree, then it was cookies with raisins in, and then it was the grocer talking to his son in a strange tongue—but even so it was wonderful. In the street the little boy kicked up his foot as he did whenever he was pleased, and began to run home with the package from the grocer's.

CHAPTER 26

THERE WILL ALWAYS BE PAIN IN THINGS

Mrs. Macauley had the kitchen table set for one, waiting for her son Homer to come to breakfast. She was setting down a bowl of oatmeal when he came into the kitchen. Her glance at him was only fleeting but even so she knew that the strange experience of his dream last night was still upon him. Even though he himself did not know he had wept in his sleep, his spirit seemed hushed as the spirit of a man is hushed after grief. Even his voice seemed deeper and gentler.

"I didn't want to sleep this late," he said. "It's

almost nine-thirty. What happened to the alarm clock?"

"You're working hard," Mrs. Macauley said. "You must rest too."

"I'm not working so hard," Homer said. "Besides, tomorrow's Sunday." He said his morning prayer, only it seemed to last twice as long as usual. Then he picked up his spoon and was about to begin to eat when he stopped and studied the spoon strangely. He looked toward his mother who was busy at the kitchen sink. "Ma?" he said.

"Yes, Homer?" Mrs. Macauley said without turning.

"I didn't talk to you last night when I came home from work," he said, "because it was like you said. I *couldn't* talk. All of a sudden on the way home last night I started to cry. You know I never did cry when I was little or at school when I was in trouble. I always felt ashamed to cry. Even Ulysses never cries because—well, what's the use crying? But last night I just couldn't help it. I cried, but I don't remember if I was ashamed even. I don't think I was. After I started to cry I couldn't come straight home. I rode out to Ithaca Wine and then, because I was still crying, I rode across town to the high school. On the way there I rode past a house where some people had been having a party earlier in the evening—the house was dark now. I took those people a telegram. You know the kind of telegram it was. Then I went back to town and rode all around the streets looking at everything—all the buildings, all the places I've known all my life, all of them full of people. And then I really saw Ithaca and I really knew the people who lived in Ithaca, all of them good people. I felt sorry for all of them and I even prayed that nothing would happen to them. After that I stopped crying. I thought a fellow would never cry when he got to be grown up, but it seems that's when a fellow starts, because that's when a fellow starts finding out about things." He stopped a moment and then his voice became even more somber than it had been. "Almost everything a man finds out is bad or sad," he said. He waited a moment for some word from his mother but she did not speak and did not turn away from her work. "Why is that so?" he said.

Mrs. Macauley began to speak, but she did not turn to him. "You will find out," she said. "No one can tell you. Each man finds out in his own way. If it's sad, nobly or foolishly, the man himself will make it so. If it's richly sad and full of beauty, it's the man himself so, and not the things around him. And so it is, if it's bad, or ugly, or pathetic—it is always the man himself, and each man *is* the world. Each man is the whole world, to make over as he will and to fill with a human race he can love, if it is love he has, or a race he must hate, if it is hate he has. The world waits to be made over by each man who inhabits it, and it is made over every morning like a bed or a household where the same people live—always the same, but always changing too." The mother was now busy on the back porch, and even though she was out of sight her son continued to speak with her.

"Why did I cry on the way home last night?" he said. "I have never felt the way I felt then. I don't understand it. And after I stopped crying why couldn't I talk? Why was there nothing for me to say—to you or to myself?"

From the porch Mrs. Macauley spoke very clearly so that he heard every word unmistakably. "It was pity that made you cry," she said. "Pity, not for this person or that person who is suffering, but for all things—for the very nature of things. Unless a man has pity he is inhuman and not yet truly a man, for out of pity comes the balm which heals. Only good men weep. If a man has not wept at the world's pain he is less than the dirt he walks upon because dirt will nourish seed, root, stalk, leaf and flower, but the spirit of a man without pity is barren and will bring forth nothing—or only pride which must finally do murder of one sort or another—murder of good *things,* or murder even of human lives." Now Mrs. Macauley returned to the sink of the kitchen where she began new work—work which even Homer knew was unnecessary.

"There will always be pain in things," Mrs. Macauley said. "Knowing this does not mean that a man shall despair. The good man will seek to take pain out of things. The foolish man will not even notice it except in himself. And the evil man will drive pain deeper into things and spread it about wherever he goes. But each man is guiltless, for the evil man no less than the foolish man or the good man did not ask to come here and did not come alone, from nothing, but from many worlds and from multitudes. The evil do not know they are evil and are therefore innocent. The evil man must be forgiven every day. He must be loved, because something of each of us is in the most evil man in the world and something of *him* is in each of us. He is ours and we are his. None of us is separate from any other. The peasant's prayer is my prayer, the assassin's crime is my crime. Last night you cried because you began to know these things."

Homer Macauley poured milk over the oatmeal in the bowl and began to eat his breakfast. Suddenly he felt it was all right to eat.

CHAPTER 27

ALL THE WONDERFUL MISTAKES

Ulysses Macauley and his best friend in the world, Lionel Cabot—the *great* Lionel—came into the Macauley kitchen. There was no mistaking this friendship, even though Lionel was a good six years older than Ulysses. They walked together and stood about together as only the very best of friends do. That is to say, easily and without much need for one or the other to speak.

"Mrs Macauley," Lionel said, "I came to ask permission—can Ulysses go to the pubalic liberry with me? I got to take back a book for my sister Lillian."

"All right, Lionel," Mrs. Macauley said. "But why aren't you with the others—with Auggie and Alf and Shag and the other boys?"

"They—" Lionel began to say and then stopped, from embarrassment. After a moment he began again. "They chased me away," he said. "They don't like me because I'm stupid." He stopped again and looked at his best friend's mother. "I'm not stupid, am I, Mrs. Macauley?"

"No, you're not, Lionel," Mrs. Macauley said. "You're the nicest boy in this neighborhood. But don't you be angry at the other boys, because they're all nice boys, too."

"I'm not angry," Lionel said. "I like every one of them. But every time I make a little mistake in a game they chase me away. They even swear at me, Mrs. Macauley. Every little mistake I make they get sore at me. 'That's all, Lionel,' they say. And when they say it, I know it's time for me to go. Sometimes I don't even last five minutes. Sometimes I make a mistake the *first* thing I do. And then they say, 'That's all, Lionel.' I don't even know what mistake I made. What do they want me to do? That's all I want to know, but nobody will tell me. Every Saturday they chase me away. Ulysses is the only one who sticks with me. He's the only partner I've got. But some day the others are going to be sorry. When the time comes and the others come to me and want me to help them—well, Mrs. Macauley, I'm going to help them, and then they're going to be sorry they chased me away all the time. Can I have a drink of water?"

"Of course, Lionel," Mrs. Macauley said. She filled a glass of water for the boy, and he drank it all down thirstily, making the kind of sound that boys make when water is still the most wonderful drink in the world.

Lionel turned to his friend. "Don't you want a drink of water, too, Ulysses?" he said.

Ulysses indicated by nodding that he would like a glass of water, so Mrs. Macauley gave him a glass, too. After he had swallowed the water, Lionel said, "Well, I guess we'll go to the pubalic liberry now, Mrs. Macauley." The two friends walked out of the house.

Homer Macauley, eating his breakfast, had watched his little brother. When the two boys were gone, he said to Mrs. Macauley, "Was Marcus like Ulysses when he was little?"

"How do you mean?" Mrs. Macauley said.

"You know," Homer said, "the way Ulysses is—interested in everything, always watching. Doesn't ever say anything but always gets a kick out of everything. Seems to like everybody and everybody seems to like him. He doesn't know many words. He can't read, but you can almost always understand him by just looking at him. You can almost even understand what he's telling you even if he doesn't say a word. Was Marcus like that too?"

"Well," Mrs. Macauley said, "Marcus and Ulysses are brothers, so of course Ulysses is something like Marcus, but they're not *exactly* alike."

"Ulysses is going to be a great man some day, isn't he, Ma?" Homer said.

"No." Mrs. Macauley smiled. "No, I don't think so—not in the eyes of the world at any rate—but he is going to be great of course, because he's great now."

"Marcus was great when he was little too, wasn't he?" Homer said.

"You've all a lot in common, of course," Mrs. Macauley said, "but not too much. Marcus was not restless as you are. He was restless, of course, but in his own way. He was shy and would rather be alone than out looking for people to see, like Ulysses. Marcus liked to read and listen to music and just sit around or go for long walks."

"Well," Homer said, "Ulysses sure likes Marcus."

"Ulysses likes everybody," Mrs. Macauley said. "He likes everybody in the world."

"Sure," Homer said, "but he likes Marcus especially, and I know why, too, because Marcus is still a child, even if he is in the Army. I guess a child looks for a child in everyone else he meets. And if he finds a child in somebody grown up, I guess he likes that person more than the others. I wish I could begin to be grown up the way Ulysses is a child. I guess I admire him more than anybody else in the world outside of our family. Did he tell you what happened to him yesterday?"

"He didn't say a word about it," Mrs. Macauley said. "Auggie came and told us."

"Well," Homer said, "what did he say when he came into the house after I brought him home from the telegraph office?"

"He didn't say anything," Mrs. Macauley said. "He just sat down, listened to the music, and then we had supper. When I put him to bed he said, 'Big Chris.' That's all, and went to sleep. I had no idea who Big Chris was until Auggie told me."

"Big Chris got Ulysses out of the trap," Homer said. "And then he paid Covington twenty dollars for the crazy invention, because it was ruined. It's *supposed* to be a trap, but I don't think it is. I don't think it could catch anybody or any *thing* in the world except Ulysses. No animal would move into something complicated like that. Who is Ulysses like —most of all?" Homer said.

"He is like his father," Mrs. Macauley said.

"Did you know Papa when he was little?" Homer said.

"Lord, no!" Mrs. Macauley said. "How could I? Your father was seven years older than me. Ulysses is like your father as your father was *all* his life." Suddenly Mrs. Macauley was filled with an overflowing feeling of happiness in spite of anything that had ever been, or anything that ever could be. "Oh, I've had good luck," she said. "and I'm thankful. My children are human beings, besides being children. They might have been children only, and then my luck would not have been so good. Last night you cried because you *are* human, because you are one of millions in the world, because the full adventure of living has started for you—in a world chock full of things that aren't easy to understand—some good, some bad, some beautiful, some ugly, some generous, and some cruel, but all of them together, *one* thing: the world and the life of men in it." She stopped a moment to look at her son. Then she said very softly, "You cried in your *sleep* last night, too."

"Did I?" Homer said. He was amazed not to have known.

"Yes," Mrs. Macauley said. "Your crying wakened Ulysses, and he came and wakened me. I heard you crying, but it was not really you."

"What do you mean?" Homer said.

"I know that sobbing," Mrs. Macauley said. "I have heard it before. It is not yours. It is not any man's. It is the whole world's. Having known the world's grief, you are now on your way, so of course all the mistakes are ahead—all the wonderful mistakes that you must and will make. I will tell you at breakfast in broad daylight what any of us might hesitate to say in the comforting darkness of night, because you are still fresh from that sleep and grief and because I *must* tell you. No matter what the mistakes are that you must make, do not be afraid of having made them or of making more of them.

Trust your heart, which is a good one, to be right, and go ahead—don't stop. If you fall, tricked or tripped by others, or by yourself even, get up and don't turn back. Many times you will laugh and many times you will weep, but always you will laugh and weep together. You will never have a moment of time in your life to be mean or petty or small. Those things will be beneath you—too small for the swiftness of your spirit—too insignificant to come into the line of your vision."

Mrs. Macauley smiled and stood beside her son, feeling a little awkward and embarrassed. "I'm sorry," she said, "that I must always, nighttime and daytime, tell you the things I know every man wants to tell himself, but I know you will forgive me."

The only thing Homer could say to this was, "Ah, Ma." He got up from the table as he spoke and limped to the window. There he looked out at the empty lot, at August Gottlieb and his pals who were in the midst of a game of football.

"What's the matter with your leg?" Mrs. Macauley said.

"Nothing," Homer said. "I took a little spill." Without turning to her, he went on. "You know, Ma, I guess you're just about the most wonderful person anybody could ever know." He began to laugh at something he saw in the football game. "There goes Auggie to another touchdown," he said. "No more games for me," he went on. "I'm going to the telegraph office. I told them I would come down just in case they need me." He turned to go, then stopped. "Oh, yes, Ma," he said, "I almost forgot. Mr. Grogan—you know, the night telegraph operator—well, he ate one of the sandwiches you sent yesterday with Bess. He told me to thank you. So thanks, Ma, for Mr. Grogan."

Homer left the house. His mother heard him bounce his bike several times to see if there was enough air in the tires, and then she saw him ride around the house headed for the telegraph office. She turned now to his chair at the table and there she saw Matthew Macauley. He was studying the spoon just as his son Homer had studied it. After a moment he looked up.

"Katey?" he said.

"Yes, Matthew?" Katey said.

"Katey," Matthew said, "Marcus is going to come with me."

There was a pause.

"I know, Matthew," Katey said, and then she turned to her work.

CHAPTER 28

AT THE PUBLIC LIBRARY

The good friends, Lionel and Ulysses, walked toward the public library. A block before them a funeral procession emerged from the First Ithaca Presbyterian Church. Pallbearers carried a plain casket to an old Packard hearse. Following the casket the two boys saw a handful of mourners.

"Come on, Ulysses," Lionel said, "it's a funeral! Somebody's dead." They ran, Lionel holding Ulysses by the hand, and very soon they were at the center of everything.

"That's the casket," Lionel whispered. "Somebody's dead in there. I wish I knew who it is. See the flowers. They give them flowers when they die. See them crying. Those are the people who knew him."

Lionel turned to a man who wasn't very busy crying. The man had just blown his nose and touched his handkerchief to the corners of his eyes.

"Who's dead?" Lionel asked the man.

"It's poor little Johnny Merryweather, the hunchback," the man said.

Lionel turned to Ulysses. "It's poor little Johnny Merryweather, the hunchback," Lionel said.

"Seventy years old," the man said.

"Seventy years old," Lionel said to Ulysses.

"Sold popcorn on the corner of Mariposa and Broadway for thirty years," the man said.

"Sold popcorn on the corner of—" Lionel stopped suddenly and looked at the man. He almost shouted. "You mean the popcorn man?" Lionel said.

"Yes," the man said, "Johnny Merryweather— gone to his rest."

"I knew *him!*" Lionel shouted. "I bought popcorn off of him many times! Did *he* die?"

"Yes," the man said, "he died peacefully. Died in his sleep. Gone to his Maker."

"I knew Johnny Merryweather!" Lionel said, almost crying. "I didn't know his name was Johnny Merryweather, but I knew him."

Lionel turned to Ulysses and put his arm around his friend. "It's Johnny," he almost wept. "Johnny

Merryweather, gone to his Maker. One of my best friends, gone to his rest."

The hearse drove away and very soon there was no one in front of the church except Lionel and Ulysses. Somehow it seemed wrong for Lionel to leave the place where he learned that the man who had died, the man in the casket, was a man he knew, even though he had never known that the man's name was Johnny Merryweather. At last, however, he decided that he couldn't stand in front of the church forever, even if he had bought popcorn off of Johnny Merryweather many times—so, thinking of the popcorn, almost tasting it again, he went on down the street with his friend Ulysses, still headed for the public library.

When the two boys entered this humble but impressive building, they entered an area of profound and almost frightening silence. It seemed as if even the walls had become speechless, and the floor and the tables, as if silence had engulfed everything in the building. There were old men reading newspapers. There were town philosophers. There were high school boys and girls doing research, but everyone was hushed, because they were seeking wisdom. They were near books. They were trying to find out. Lionel not only whispered, he moved on tiptoe. Lionel whispered because he was under the impression that it was out of respect for books, not consideration for readers. Ulysses followed him, also on tiptoe, and they explored the library, each finding many treasures, Lionel—books, and Ulysses—people. Lionel didn't read books and he hadn't come to the public library to get any for himself. He just liked to *see* them—the thousands of them. He pointed out a whole row of shelved books to his friend and then he whispered, "All of these—and these. And these. Here's a red one. All these. There's a green one. All these."

Finally Mrs. Gallagher, the old librarian, noticed the two boys and went over to them. *She* didn't whisper, however. She spoke right out, as if she were not in the public library at all. This shocked Lionel and made a few people look up from the pages of their books.

"What are you looking for, boy?" Mrs. Gallagher said to Lionel.

"Books," Lionel whispered softly.

"What books are you looking for?" the librarian said.

"All of them," Lionel said.

"All of them?" the librarian said. "What do you mean? You can't borrow more than four books on one card."

"I don't want to borrow *any* of them," Lionel said.

"Well, what in the world *do* you want with them?" the librarian said.

"I just want to look at them," Lionel said.

"Look at them?" the librarian said. "That is not

what the public library is for. You can look *into* them, you can look *at* the pictures in them, but what in the world do you want to look at the outsides of them for?"

"I like to," Lionel whispered. "Can't I?"

"Well," the librarian said, "there's no law against it." She looked at Ulysses. "And who's this?" she said.

"This here's Ulysses," Lionel said. "He can't read."

"Can you?" the librarian said to Lionel.

"No," Lionel said, "but he can't either. That's why we're friends. He's the only other man I know who can't read."

The old librarian looked at the two friends a moment and in her mind said something which very nearly approached a kind of delicious cursing. This was something brand new in all the years of her experience at the public library. "Well," she said at last, "perhaps it's just as well that you *can't* read. *I* can read. I have been reading books for the past sixty years, and I can't see as how it's made any great difference. Run along now and look at the books as you please."

"Yes, ma'am," Lionel said.

The two friends moved off into still greater realms of mystery and adventure. Lionel pointed out more books to Ulysses. "These," he said. "And those over there. And these. All books, Ulysses." He stopped a moment to think. "I wonder what they say in all these books." He pointed out a whole vast area of them, five shelves full of them. "All these," he said— "I wonder what they say." Finally he discovered a book that looked very pretty from the outside. Its cover was green, like fresh grass. "And this one," he said, "this one is pretty, Ulysses."

A little frightened at what he was doing, Lionel lifted the book out of the shelf, held it in his hands a moment and then opened it. "There, Ulysses!" he said. "A book! There it is! See? They're saying something in here." Now he pointed to something in the print of the book. "There's an 'A,' " he said. "That's an 'A' right there. There's another letter of some sort. I don't know what that one is. Every letter's different, Ulysses, and every word's different." He sighed and looked around at all the books. "I don't think I'll ever learn to read," he said, "but I sure would like to know what they're saying in there. Now here's a picture," he said. "Here's a picture of a girl. See her? Pretty, isn't she?" He turned many pages of the book and said, "See it? More letters and words, straight through to the end of the book. This is the pubalic liberry, Ulysses," he said. "Books all over the place." He looked at the print of the book with a kind of reverence, whispering to himself as if he were trying to read. Then he shook his head. "You can't know what a book says, Ulysses, unless you can read, and I can't read," he said.

He closed the book slowly, put it back in its place, and together the two friends tiptoed out of the library. Outside, Ulysses kicked up his heel because he felt good, and because it seemed he had learned something new.

CHAPTER 29

AT THE PARLOR LECTURE
CLUB

Homer Macauley got off his bicycle in front of
the Ithaca Parlor Lecture Club, a white building
which was an architectural cross between a Colonial
house and a New England church. It was now two-
thirty in the afternoon and this Saturday afternoon's lecture was about to begin. Consequently,
wonderful, plump, vague, middle-aged ladies, most
of them mothers, were cheerfully entering the building. The messenger took a telegram out of his hat
and studied it. The telegram was addressed to

Rosalie Simms-Peabody, Ithaca Parlor Lecture Club, Ithaca, California. Deliver in person.

As the messenger walked into the hall, the President of the Club, a sweet and roundish lady in her early fifties, was beginning to introduce the lecturer, who was nowhere to be seen. The President of the Club pounded a small walnut-breaker on the table and the audience in the hall began to quiet down. Homer Macauley, however, could not help making a small amount of noise by seeking Rosalie Simms-Peabody. Therefore, a sweetly smiling lady of perhaps one hundred and sixty pounds shushed him.

"I've got a telegram for Rosalie Simms-Peabody," Homer whispered. "It's to be delivered to her *personally.*"

"Rosalie Simms-*Pibity,*" the lady corrected the messenger. "Yes, Rosalie Simms-Pibity is expecting the telegram. You are to deliver it to her on the platform when she appears."

"When is that going to be?" Homer said.

"In a moment now," the lady said. "Just sit down and wait. When Rosalie Simms-Pibity appears, run right up onto the stage and call out very clearly, 'Telegram for Rosalie Simms-Pibity!' Not *Peabody,* boy."

"Yes, ma'am," Homer said. The messenger sat down and the lady tiptoed away, smiling proudly at the important work she had done.

"Members of the Ithaca Parlor Lecture Club," the President of the Club began to say. "This afternoon," she continued, "we have in store a great treat. Our speaker is to be Rosalie Simms-Pibity." The President of the Club paused after the announcement of this name so that there would be time for the customary applause. After the applause, she continued. "I do not have to tell you who Rosalie Simms-Pibity is," she said. "She is internationally famous—one of the great women of our time. We all know her name and we all know she is famous. But do we, I wonder, know *why* she is famous." The President of the Club answered this question. "I am afraid not," she said. And then after a moment of looking about at her friends in the audience, the women of Ithaca, California, she began the fable of this great person. "The story of Rosalie Simms-Pibity," the President of the Club said, as if she were telling a fable not the least unlike, or not one bit less majestic than the fable of the Odyssey itself, "is a story *especially* thrilling to women. Simms-Pibity—for that is how she prefers to be known—has lived a life brimming over with adventure, romance, danger, and beauty, and yet today she is scarcely more than a dashing handsome British *girl*—at the same time a girl hard as steel and stronger than most men. In fact, there are few men who have lived a life as adventurous as the life of Simms-Pibity."

Now a note of tender sadness came into the voice of the President of the Ithaca Parlor Lecture Club as she continued the legend of the great female hero. "As for us," she said somberly, "the stay-at-homes, the mothers, the bringer-uppers, so to speak, of children, the life of Simms-Pibity is like a dream—*our* dream—the unfulfilled dream of each of us who have only stayed at home, given birth to our children, and looked after our houses. Hers is the beautiful life each of us would have *liked* to have lived if we had dared, but Fate, as it will, has not decreed such adventures for us, and in all the world there is only one Simms-Pibity. Only one!"

The President of the Club again paused to look over the faces of her old friends in the audience. "What is it," she said, "that Simms-Pibity has done which has made her so rare among women? Well," she went on, "the list of her adventures is staggering, and as I read the list to you, you will scarcely be able to believe any woman could do such things and still be alive, but alive she is, and here to talk to us. Simms-Pibity is going to talk to us in plain language—language perhaps, to some of us, shocking. But first let me go over the adventures—only briefly —for a full recitation of them would take all day and perhaps all night, as *every* day is a new adventure for Simms-Pibity. She *creates* adventure wherever she goes, and we may be sure that before she leaves our unknown little city, Ithaca, she will have discovered here things we ourselves do not know. But on to the adventures.

"From 1915 to 1917 Simms-Pibity drove an ambulance at the front—in the other war. During 1917 and 1918 she went around the world with another girl—on tramp steamers, cattle boats, walking and riding and living in many strange places—sometimes even in native huts. She visited twenty-seven different countries. She was captured by the Southern Army in China as she tried to go overland by river junk and sedan chair from Canton to Hankow." The President of the Club paused a moment to dwell on the magical words, and then repeated them, almost whispering. "Canton and Hankow. Simms-Pibity escaped her capturers by shooting the falls of the Sian River in the wet season when no other boat would go out on them.

"In 1919 she went across North Africa from Morocco to Abyssinia. In 1920 she was employed in Syria in the secret service. In Damascus she met King Feisal, who helped her make the exploration of Kufara, never before visited by white people, the secret and sacred capital of the fanatic Senussi Sect, deep in the heart of the Libyan Desert. Simms-Pibity went disguised as an Egyptian woman one thousand miles on camel-back, her only companions coarse, native men who could speak no English." The President of the Ithaca Parlor Lecture Club lifted her eyes after this remark and looked over at two of her most intimate friends. Homer Macauley wondered what she meant by that glance and then wondered how long she was going to talk about this incredible and wonderful person, Rosalie Simms-Pibity.

"During 1923," the speaker continued, "Simms-

Pibity sailed a twenty-ton dhow with an Arab crew fourteen days down the Red Sea to land at the forbidden port of Jeizan. This time she was disguised as an Arab woman. In 1925 she climbed the Atlas Mountains of Morocco. In 1926 she walked one thousand one hundred miles through Abyssinia—perhaps a world record." And then with terrible scorn for herself and her friends in Ithaca, the President of the Ithaca Parlor Lecture Club said, "Do we, I wonder, ever walk with pleasure even so short a distance as the distance from Gottschalk's to Roeding Park?" She sighed and then, not knowing how to answer this question, she offered, "It might perhaps do us good." She returned to the matter of introducing the lecturer of the day, looking for her place in the booklet of notes she held in her hand.

"To continue," she said. "In 1928 Simms-Pibity covered the Balkans for a London newspaper, disguised now as a native woman of one country, now as a native woman of another."

Getting bored, waiting impatiently, eager to get back to the telegraph office and his work, Homer Macauley wondered, "Why is she always disguising herself?"

The President of the Ithaca Parlor Lecture Club went on with her introduction. "In 1930," she said, "Simms-Pibity made an exciting journey through Turkey and met Mustapha Kemal, a Turk. There Simms-Pibity was disguised as a young Turkish girl from the hill country. She traveled over nine thousand miles on horseback, moving all through the Near East. In Azerbaijan she saw the uprising between the Communist Red Army and the Caucasian peasants. In 1931 she traveled through South America, exploring the jungles of Brazil with only native men for companions, one of whom was named, I understand—from Simms-Pibity herself—Max." The President of the Ithaca Parlor Lecture Club was now close to the end of her speech of introduction. She sighed and said, "But the adventures of Simms-Pibity are endless, and it is *her* you wish to see and hear, not *me*." This sweet modesty brought a nervous giggle out of the wonderful President of the wonderful Club, and then a kind of sympathetic but hearty laughter from her friends in the audience. When a proper quietude had come over the audience, the President said in a firm and dramatic voice, "It gives me great pride, as President of the Ithaca Parlor Lecture Club, to present to you—Rosalie Simms-Pibity!"

The applause this time was almost an ovation. The President of the Club turned toward the wings of the stage to greet the distinguished visitor, but alas, the visitor was nowhere to be seen. The audience, taking advantage of this delay, increased its applause and after perhaps two full minutes of clapping—during which a number of women actually confessed that their hands were getting sore—the great lady finally presented herself.

The Human Comedy

Homer Macauley expected to see somebody unlike any woman he had ever seen before in his life. He couldn't imagine exactly what form this creature would take, but he felt certain that it would be surely at least interesting—and so it was. Rosalie Simms-Pibity was, briefly, an old battle-ax, horse-faced, sex-starved, dried-out, tall, skinny, gaunt, bony, absurd, and a mess. Because the time had come for Homer to deliver the telegram, he got to his feet, but he was not sure he didn't get to his feet because he was amazed, and it was strange that he did not run up onto the stage and deliver the telegram, as he had been instructed to do.

Now the nice lady who had given him his instructions came rushing over, and before he knew it she was pushing him down the aisle and whispering loud enough for everyone to hear, "Now, boy—now! Deliver the telegram!"

On the stage the great lady pretended not to be aware of this commotion. "Ladies," she began to say. "Members of the Ithaca Parlor Lecture Club—" Her voice was equal in unattractiveness to her person.

Homer Macauley hurried up onto the stage and in a very clear voice announced, "Telegram for Rosalie Simms-Pibity!"

The great lady stopped her speech and turned to the messenger as if his appearance was utterly accidental. "Here, boy," she said, "I am Simms-Pibity!"

She glanced back at the audience and said, "Excuse me, ladies." She signed for the telegram, took it from the messenger, and then offered him a dime, saying, "And that's for you, boy."

This was painful to Homer but at the same time everything had been so ridiculous and confusing that he did not care to bother about refusing. He took the small coin and, very much embarrassed, hurried down from the stage and out of the building. As he hurried he could hear the woman beginning her speech.

"Now, in 1939," she said, "just before the outbreak of this new War, I chanced to be in Bavaria on a secret mission, disguised as an Alsatian milkmaid."

In the street, seated on the sidewalk, Homer saw Henry Wilkinson who had lost both legs in a railway accident when he was a young man. Now, thirty years later, he had taken to holding a hat in his lap containing pencils. Homer did not know him by name but had seen him all his life. Somehow or other he had never gotten around to buying a pencil or dropping a coin into the hat. The dime from Rosalie Simms-Pibity had already become an object of which he wished to be rid. Therefore, upon seeing Henry Wilkinson, Homer dropped the dime into the man's hat and hurried to his bicycle. He had swung onto his bicycle and had gone twenty yards down the street when he decided that something was wrong with what he had done, so he turned around and hurried back, dropped his bicycle on the sidewalk and ran over to the man who had lost his legs thirty years ago, and this time Homer dropped a quarter—his own—into the hat.

CHAPTER 30

MR. MECHANO

After their adventure in the public library, Lionel and Ulysses continued to explore Ithaca. At sundown they found themselves standing at the very front of a small crowd of idlers and passers-by, watching a man in the window of a third-rate drug store. The man moved like a piece of machinery, although he *was* a human being. He looked, however, as if he had been made of wax instead of flesh. He seemed inhuman and in fact he looked like nothing so much as an upright, unburied corpse still capable of moving. The man was the most incredible thing Ulysses had seen in all of his four years of life in the world.

No light came out of the man's eyes. His lips were set as if they would never part.

The man was engaged in advertising *Dr. Bradford's Tonic*. He worked between two easels. On one easel was a sign on which this message had been printed: "Mr. Mechano—The Machine Man—Half Machine, Half Human. More Dead Than Alive. $50 if you can make him smile. $500 if you can make him laugh." On the other easel Mr. Mechano placed pasteboard cards which he took in an extremely mechanical fashion from the small table in front of the easel. On these cards were printed various messages urging people to buy the patent medicine which Dr. Bradford had invented and thereby to become more alive. After each new card had been placed on the easel Mr. Mechano pointed at each word of the message on the card with a pointer. When all ten of the cards had been placed on the easel, Mr. Mechano removed them all and put them back on the table and began the procedure all over again.

"It's a man, Ulysses," Lionel said to his friend. "I can see him. It's not a machine, Ulysses. It's a man! See his eyes? He's alive. See him?"

The card Mr. Mechano had just placed on the easel read: "Don't drag yourself around half dead. Enjoy life. Take Dr. Bradford's Tonic and feel like a new man."

"There's another card," Lionel said. "It says something on that card." Suddenly he was weary and eager to get home. "Come on, Ulysses," he said, "let's go. We've seen him go through all the cards three times. Let's go home. It's almost night now." He took his friend by the hand, but Ulysses drew his hand away.

"Come on, Ulysses!" Lionel said. "I've got to go home now. I'm hungry." But Ulysses did not want to go. It seemed that he did not even *hear* Lionel's words.

"I'm going, Ulysses," Lionel challenged. He waited for Ulysses to turn and go with him, but the boy did not budge. A little hurt and amazed by this betrayal of friendship, Lionel began to walk home, turning every three or four steps to see if his friend was not going to join him after all. But no, Ulysses wanted to stay and watch Mr. Mechano. Lionel felt deeply wounded as he continued his journey home. "I thought he was my best friend in the whole world," he said.

Ulysses stood among the handful of people watching Mr. Mechano until at last only he and an old man were left. Mr. Mechano went right on picking up the cards and putting them on the easel. He went right on pointing to each word on each card. Soon the old man went away too, and then only Ulysses stood on the sidewalk looking up at the strange human being in the window of the drug store. It was growing dark now. When the street lights came on, Ulysses came out of the trance of fascination into which the vision of Mr. Mechano had placed him.

It was almost as if he had become hypnotized by the sight of the man. Now, out of the trance, he looked around. Day had ended and everybody had gone— The only thing left anywhere was something for which he had no word—Death.

The small boy looked back suddenly at the mechanical man. It seemed then that the man was looking at *him*. There was swift and fierce terror in the boy. Suddenly he was running away. The few people he saw in the streets now seemed full of death, too, like Mr. Mechano. They seemed suddenly ugly, not beautiful, as they had always seemed before. Ulysses ran until he was almost exhausted. He stopped, breathing hard and almost crying. He looked around, feeling a deep silent steady horror in all things—the horror of Mr. Mechano—Death! He had never before known fear of *any* kind, let alone fear such as this, and it was the most difficult thing in the world for him to know what to do. His poise was all gone—scattered by the fear of the horror catching up with *him,* and he began to run again. This time as he ran he said to himself, almost crying, "Papa, Mama, Marcus, Bess, Homer! Papa, Mama, Marcus, Bess, Homer!"

The world was surely wonderful and it was surely full of good things to be seen again and again, but now the world was a thing to escape, only he could think of no direction to take. He wanted swiftly to reach somebody of his family. He stood panic-stricken, and then began moving a few steps in one

direction and then a few in another, feeling all
around him a presence of incredible disaster, a disaster he could escape only by reaching his father, his
mother, one of his brothers, or his sister. And then,
instead of reaching one of these, he saw far down the
street the leader of the neighborhood gang, August
Gottlieb. The newsboy was standing on a deserted
street corner, calling out the headline as if the area
around him were full of people who must be told
what had happened that day in the world. Hollering
headlines had always seemed slightly ridiculous to
August Gottlieb because, for one thing, the headlines were always about murder of one sort or another and, for another, because it seemed somehow a
thing of bad taste to go about among people in the
streets of Ithaca lifting his voice. Consequently, the
newsboy felt pleased when at last he discovered that
the streets were deserted. Without even knowing
that he was doing such a thing, whenever the streets
had become empty of the people of Ithaca, August
Gottlieb, as if grateful for his almost solitary in-
habitance of the city, lifted his voice more power-
fully than ever, calling out the day's miserable news.
What could a man do about the news—sell a paper,
and make a few pennies? Is that what he could do
about it? Wasn't it foolish for him to cry out the daily
message of mistake as if it were glad tidings? Wasn't
it shameful for the people to be so steadily unim-
pressed with the nature of every day's news? Sometimes even in his sleep the newsboy dreamed of call-

ing out the headlines of the world's news, but there, in that inner area of experience, he felt mockery and contempt for the nature of the news, and when he shouted, it was always from a great height, and beneath him always were multitudes engaged in activities of error and crime. But the minute they heard his roaring voice, they stopped in their tracks to look up at him, and then he always shouted, "Now go back, go back where you belong! Stop your murder! Plant trees instead!" He had always loved the idea of planting a tree.

When Ulysses saw August Gottlieb on the street corner, much of the terror in his heart passed away and he began to feel that it would not be years and years before he might again find goodness and love in the world. The little boy wanted to shout out to August Gottlieb, but he couldn't make a sound. Instead, he ran with all his might to the newsboy and flung himself upon him in an embrace so forceful that it almost knocked Auggie down.

"Ulysses!" the newsboy said. "What's the matter? What are you crying about?"

Ulysses looked up into the eyes of the newsboy, but still he could not speak.

"You're scared, Ulysses," Auggie said. "Well, don't be scared—there's nothing to be scared of. Now don't cry, Ulysses. You don't have to be scared." But still the boy could not stop sobbing. "Now don't cry any more," Auggie said, and waited for Ulysses to stop. Ulysses tried very hard not to cry and soon the sobs came at infrequent intervals, each sob like a hiccup. Then Auggie said, "Come on, Ulysses, we'll go to Homer."

At the sound of that name, the name of his brother, Ulysses smiled, and then hiccuped another sob. "Homer?" he said.

"Sure," Auggie said. "Your brother. Come on."

It was almost too wonderful for the little boy to believe. "Going to see Homer?" he said.

"Sure," Auggie said. "The telegraph office is just around the corner."

August Gottlieb and Ulysses Macauley walked around the corner to the telegraph office. They found Homer seated at the delivery desk. When Ulysses saw his brother, a wonderful thing happened to his face. All the terror left his eyes, because now he was home.

When Homer saw his brother, he got up and went to the boy and lifted him in his arms. He turned to Auggie. "What's the matter?" he said. "What's Ulysses doing in town at this hour?"

"He got lost, I guess," Auggie said. "He was crying."

"Crying?" Homer said, and then hugged his brother, just as Ulysses hiccuped another sob. "All right, Ulysses," he said. "Don't cry any more. I'll take you home on my bike. Now, don't cry."

From his desk the manager of the telegraph office, Thomas Spangler, watched the three boys, and the old telegraph operator, William Grogan, stopped his work to watch them, too. They looked at one another several times. Homer put his brother down. He knew the boy was all right again when Ulysses went to the delivery desk to look at things there. Ulysses was always all right if he was interested in things, and now he was interested again. Homer put his arm around August and said, "Thanks, Auggie. It would have been terrible if he didn't find you."

Spangler got up and went to the two boys. "Hello, Auggie," he said. "Let me have a paper."

"Yes, sir," Auggie said, and began to go through the routine of folding the paper and making the sale, but Spangler stopped him so that he could hold the paper up before him. The manager of the telegraph office glanced at the headline, and then threw the paper into the wastebasket. "How's it going, Auggie?" he said.

"Not bad, Mr. Spangler," Auggie said. "I've made fifty-five cents so far today, but I started selling papers at one o'clock this afternoon. When I make seventy-five cents I'm going home."

"Why?" Spangler said. "Why do you want to make seventy-five cents?"

"I don't know," Auggie said. "I just thought I ought to make seventy-five cents on a Saturday. There's nobody in town hardly, but I think I can sell the rest of my papers in another hour or two. Pretty soon people start coming back to town after supper—the movie crowd."

"Well," Spangler said, "to hell with the movie crowd. You give me the rest of your papers and go on home *now*. Here's a quarter."

Even though the newsboy felt deeply grateful to the manager of the telegraph office for this gesture, somehow it didn't seem right to him. You had to sell papers one at a time and each one to a different person, and you had to stand on a street corner and holler the headline and make the people *want* to read the news. But even so, he was tired, and he wanted to get home to supper, and he never did know anybody like Spangler before, and maybe Spangler wanting to buy all his papers at once to throw into the wastebasket was the best news of the whole day anyway. It just didn't seem right that it should be a good man like Spangler, though, instead of the riffraff of the streets—well, maybe not exactly riffraff, but whatever they were. The newsboy felt that he would have to protest a sale of this sort. "I don't want to make a quarter from *you,* Mr. Spangler," he said.

"Never mind," Spangler said. "Give me the papers and go home."

"Yes, sir," Auggie said. "But maybe you'll let me do something for you to make up for this quarter some day."

"Sure, sure," Spangler said, and threw the papers into the wastebasket.

Auggie turned to Ulysses who was now studying

the call box on the delivery desk. "Ulysses got lost," Auggie said to Mr. Spangler.

"Well," Spangler said, "he's not lost now. Ulysses!" he called out to the boy, and Ulysses turned to look at the manager of the telegraph office. After a moment, finding nothing appropriate to say to the boy, Spangler said, "How are you?" And after a moment, Ulysses, finding nothing appropriate to say in reply to this question said, "O.K." Each of them knew that something else had been meant.

Homer said, knowing it was the wrong thing, "He's O.K." And then Auggie, purely out of confusion, repeated these two words, as if he meant a whole new wonderful bright meaning. They all felt awkward, but very happy, especially Spangler.

William Grogan, the telegraph operator, after this exchange of ideas, brought out his bottle, unscrewed the cap, and took a good long swig.

Auggie turned to go home, but Homer stopped him. "Wait a minute, Auggie," he said, "I'll hike you home. Is it all right, Mr. Spangler? I've got a pickup at Ithaca Wine, and it's on the way home. So if it's all right, I'll hike Ulysses and Auggie home and then go and get the pickup at Ithaca Wine. Is it all right?"

"Sure, sure," Spangler said, and went back to his desk. He picked up the hard-boiled egg which he believed brought him good luck—or at least kept away anything like extremely bad luck.

Mr. Mechano

"No," Auggie said to Homer. "You don't need to hike me home. Hiking two people at once on a bike is too much, Homer. I can walk it in no time."

"I'll hike you home," Homer said. "You can't walk it in no time. It's almost three miles. I can hike both of you very easily. You can sit on the frame and Ulysses can sit on the handlebars. Now come on."

The three boys went out to Homer's bicycle. The load was a heavy one, especially for a man with one bad leg, but Homer got his passengers home all right. They stopped first at the little house next door to Ara's Market—Auggie's house. Ara himself was standing in front of his store, holding the hand of his little boy. They were looking up into the sky. Down the street, next to the empty lot, Mrs. Macauley stood in the yard under the old walnut tree, taking clothes off the line. Mary and Bess were in the parlor playing and singing, and the sound of the piano and Mary's voice could be heard faintly.

Auggie got off the bicycle and went into his house. Homer stood a moment in the street, holding the bike and looking up at the sky and over at the Macauley house. Then, Auggie came out of the house and went up to Ara, the grocer.

"Did you do a lot of business today, Mr. Ara?" Auggie said to the grocer.

"Thank you, Auggie," the grocer said. "I am satisfied."

"I've got seventy-five cents I want to spend," Auggie said. "I want to get a lot of things for to-morrow."

"All right, Auggie," the grocer said, but before turning to go back into the store he pointed to the clouds in the sky and then looked at his son. "See, John?" he said. "Nighttime come now—pretty soon we get in our beds, go to sleep. Sleep all night. When daytime come, we get up again. New day."

The grocer and his son and the neighbor boy went into the store. In the meantime, Ulysses, sitting on the handlebars of his brother's bicycle, was watching his mother. Now Homer got back onto the bicycle and began to ride toward the house.

"Mama," Ulysses said to his brother, turning to look up into his face.

"Sure," Homer said. "That's Mama right over there in the yard under the tree. See her?"

As they came closer to the woman in the yard under the tree, the little brother's face grew full of a smiling light, but at the same time there was now a deep sadness in that face and in the face of the brother who held the handlebars, almost embracing him.

Homer rode straight across the empty lot into the backyard, under the walnut tree. He got off the bicycle and set Ulysses down on his feet. Ulysses stood looking at his mother. Gone from him now almost as if forever was the terror that had come from Mr. Mechano.

226

"He got lost, Ma," Homer said. "Auggie found him and brought him to the telegraph office. I can't stay, but I'll go in and say hello to Bess and Mary."

Homer went into the house and stood in the dark dining room, listening to his sister and the girl his brother loved. When the song was over, he moved into the parlor. "Hello," he said.

The two girls turned. "Hello, Homer," Mary said, and then very swiftly, with great happiness, "I got a letter from Marcus today."

"Did you, Mary?" Homer said. "How is he?"

"Just fine," Mary said. "They're going away soon, but they don't know where. He says not to worry if we don't get any more letters for a while."

"He wrote to all of us," Bess said, "to Mama, and me, and even to Ulysses."

"Did he?" Homer said. He waited a moment for the announcement of the arrival of *his* letter, afraid there might not be any such announcement. At last he said very quietly, "Didn't he send *me* a letter, too?"

"Oh, of course," Mary said. "Yours is the biggest letter of all. I thought you would know that if he wrote to all of us, he would write to you, too."

Homer's sister lifted a letter off the table and handed it to him. Homer looked at the letter a long time and then his sister said, "Well, why don't you open it and read it? Read it to us."

"No, Bess," Homer said. "I've got to go now.

I'll take it to the office and read it there tonight when I've got a lot of time."

"We spent the whole day looking for a job," Bess said, "but we didn't find one."

"We had a lot of fun just the same, Bess," Mary said. "It was a lot of fun just going in and asking."

"Well, fun or no fun," Homer said, "I'm glad you didn't find a job. Never mind a job. I make all the money we need, and Mary's father's got a good job at Ithaca Wine. You two don't need to go looking for a job."

"Yes, we do, Homer," Bess said. "Sure we do. And one of these days we're going to find ourselves a job. Two places asked us to come back."

"Never mind finding a job," Homer said. He was angry now. "You don't have to find a job, Bess, or you, Mary. Any work that has to be done around here, men can do. Girls belong in homes, taking care of men, that's all—just play the piano and sing and look pretty for a fellow to see when he comes home. That's all you need to do." He stopped a moment and when he spoke again he spoke gently, turning to Mary. "When Marcus comes home," he said, "you two can rent a little house of your own and start bringing up a family, the way you want to." He turned to Bess. "And one of these days, Bess, you'll find a guy you like. That's the only job you ought to be thinking about. Just because there happens to be a war in the world isn't a reason for everybody to go out of their heads. Just stay home where you belong and help Mama, and you help your father, Mary."

He was so bossy, his sister Bess was almost proud of him, because never before had she seen him so concerned about *anything.*

"And don't forget it," Homer said to his sister and to the neighbor girl. "Now," he said, "play another song before I go."

"What song would you like to hear?" Bess said.

"Any song," Homer said.

Homer's sister Bess began to play a song and soon Mary began to sing. The messenger stood in the dark of the parlor listening and before the song was half finished he went quietly out of the house. Now, in the yard, he found Ulysses standing over the hen nest looking down at one egg.

"Ma," Homer said. His mother turned to him. "Tomorrow be sure we all go to church. All of us together—and Mary."

"Why, what do you mean, Homer?" Mrs. Macauley said. "We go to church almost *every* Sunday, and Mary is almost *always* with us."

"I know," Homer said almost impatiently. "But tomorrow, for *sure.* And with Mary, for *sure.*" He turned to his brother and said, "What have you got there in your hand, Ulysses?"

"Egg," Ulysses said as if the word were also the word for God.

Homer got onto his bicycle and began riding toward Ithaca Wine.

CHAPTER 31

LEANING ON THE EVER-LASTING ARMS

As Homer rode his bicycle toward the winery, far away, so far that even the hour of day was different from the hour in Ithaca, an American passenger train moved swiftly over American earth through an American night. The train was filled with American boys, among them Marcus and his friend Tobey —all of them dressed as soldiers and trained for war. But from their eyes, from their high spirits, and from their laughter and shouting and singing, you knew this was not an army alone, but a nation, and surely a good and great one. You knew that while they had been taught to stand in line and to behave on schedule with no personal rights beyond the needs of the unit, they had not become a machine and were still good human beings with at least average intentions. You knew that if they were noisy and perhaps unaware of their own importance, they were not without dignity. You knew surely that while their noise came from deep inner fear, they were still utterly unafraid. You knew they had accepted for no terribly pompous or false reasons the necessity to dismiss their fear, and if it so happened, to die. You knew they were American boys, some of them past forty even, but most of them kids—kids from big cities and little towns, from farms and offices, from rich families and poor families, kids lifted out of great worlds and kids lifted out of small worlds, some moved away from magnificent dreams of action and some from humble dreams of peace— kids brilliant and swift in spirit and kids slow and steady. In the midst of the clamor, the laughter, the excitement, the confusion, the eagerness, and the magnificent combination of profound ignorance and profound wisdom, Marcus Macauley and his friend Tobey George talked quietly.

"Well," Tobey said, "I guess we're on our way."

"That's right," Marcus said.

"You know, Marcus," Tobey said, "I feel lucky, because if it hadn't been for this War I wouldn't have run into you and I would never have found out about your family."

Marcus felt embarrassed. "Thanks," he said. "I feel the same way about you." He stopped a moment and then asked the question that every man exposed to unknown danger must ask himself again and again. "I want you to tell me the truth," he said. "Are you going to care much if you're killed?"

The other could not answer the question immediately, but at last he said, "Sure. I *could* bluff, I guess, and *pretend* that I wouldn't care. Of course I'm going to care. Aren't you?"

"Yes," Marcus said. "I'm going to care very much. I just wanted to know." He stopped a moment and then said, "What do you *think* about? What do you want to get back to?"

"I don't know," Tobey said, because he didn't know. "I guess I want to get back to—well, anything—whatever it happens to be. I haven't got a family as you have. I haven't anybody to go back to, but whatever it is, that'll be O.K. with me. I want to get back to whatever it turns out to be. I haven't got a girl waiting for me like your girl Mary, but I know I want to get back just the same—if I can."

"Sure," Marcus said.

Again they were silent a moment and then Marcus said, "How does it happen that you like to sing?"

"How should I know?" Tobey said. "I just like to sing, that's all." They listened to the train and to the noise inside the train and then Tobey said, "What do *you* think about?"

Leaning on the Everlasting Arms

Marcus took a little time before beginning to answer this question. "I think about my father," he said, "and my mother, and my sister Bess and my brother Homer and my brother Ulysses. And I think about Mary and her father, Mr. Arena. I think about the whole neighborhood, the empty lot, the kids, the houses, Ara's Market, and Ara himself. The railroad tracks where I used to watch the trains go by, the Sunday School, the church, the courthouse park, the Public Library, the old teachers, the kids who used to be in my life—some of them dead already, but not from this War—just dead."

"It's a funny thing," Tobey said. "Maybe you won't understand a thing like this, but I feel that Ithaca is *my* home town, too." He waited a moment and then said, "If we get through all right, if we come out of this O.K., will you take me with you to Ithaca? Will you show me the places you knew, and tell me about them, what happened at this place and what happened at that place?"

"Sure," Marcus said, "sure. I *want* to do that. And I want you to meet my family, too. We're poor, always have been—my father was a *great* man. He was not a successful man. He didn't make any more money than what we needed—ever."

"Matthew Macauley?" Tobey said.

"Yes," Marcus said. "Matthew Macauley, my father. He worked in the vineyards, in the packing houses, and in the wineries. He did plain, ordinary, everyday work. If you saw him in the street you would think he was nobody. He looked like anybody else and acted like anybody else—but even so he was a great man. He was my father and I know he was great. The only thing he cared about was his family—my mother and his children. He saved money for months and made a down payment on a harp—yes, a harp—I know nobody plays a harp any more but that's what my mother wanted, so my father saved up money and made a down payment on a harp for her. It took him five years to pay for the harp. It was the most expensive harp you could buy. We used to think every house had a harp just because we had one. Then he bought a piano for my sister Bess—that didn't cost so much. I thought everybody was great like my father—until I got out and met some of the rest of the people. They're all right, they're fine—but I don't think they're great. Well, maybe they *are* and I just don't know them very well. You've got to know people real well to know whether they're great or not. A lot of people are great that nobody ever thinks are great."

"I wish I knew a man like your father," Tobey said. "Of course he wouldn't have to be *my* father. He could be anybody, just so I *knew* him. I guess I'm lucky in a way, not knowing who my father was, because, not knowing, I can *believe* he was great, just like your father."

"Maybe he *was* great," Marcus said.

"Maybe," Tobey said. "I hope so. You know, I didn't know kids had mothers and fathers until I went to school and heard the other kids talk about them." Tobey laughed with embarrassment. "I couldn't understand it," he said. "I thought every man was in the world alone—the same as me—to start out all by himself. I guess I felt bad for a long time, after I found out. It made me lonely. I mean it made me *lonelier*. Maybe *that's* the reason I like to sing. You don't feel your loneliness so much when you're singing." Then shyly, almost timidly, he said, "What kind of a girl is Bess?"

Marcus knew his friend was uncomfortable asking this question and he didn't want him to be uncomfortable. "That's all right," Marcus said. "You can ask me about my sister. I want you to meet her. I think she will like you."

"Me?" Tobey said.

"Yes, I have an idea she might like you very much," Marcus said. "I want to take you back and have you stay at our house. If you like each other— well, I guess Bess is just about—well, anyway, even if she *is* my sister—well, I just think she'll like you very much, that's all."

Now Marcus began to speak very swiftly, because while he knew it was almost impossible to speak of such a thing at all, he also knew it was necessary to *try* to do so at least. Therefore he wanted to get the words spoken and their meaning established as swiftly as possible so that his embarrassment would not endure too long. "Marry her and live in Ithaca," he said. "It's a good town. You'll be happy there.

Now, here. I'm going to give you her picture—to keep." He handed Tobey a little snapshot of his sister Bess. "Keep it in your identification folder where I keep Mary's picture. See?"

Tobey George took the photograph of his friend's sister and looked at it for a long time, while Marcus looked at him. At last he said, "Bess sure is beautiful. I don't know if a guy can fall in love with a girl without meeting her, but I feel in love with Bess already. I feel sick. I'll tell you the truth. I was afraid to talk to you about Bess until now. But I figured, well, maybe as long as we're on our way, and there's no telling, you might not mind so much. I can't help it, but I always feel I haven't the same kind of rights that other people have—you know, a guy who is given his name by an orphanage, not by his mother and father—who doesn't even know who his mother and father were—who doesn't even know what nationality they were—or what nationality *he* is. Some people say I'm Spanish and French, and some people say I'm Italian and Greek, and some people say I'm English and Irish. Almost everybody gives me a different nationality."

"You're an American," Marcus said. "That's all. Any man can see that."

"Sure," Tobey said. "I guess that's right, all right. I guess I'm an American all right. But I sure would like to know *which* American."

"You're the American whose name is Tobey George," Marcus said. "That's good enough for anybody. Now keep that picture. We'll go back to Ithaca and you'll raise a family and I'll raise a family, and we'll visit each other once in a while, have some music and songs—pass the time of life."

"You know, Marcus," Tobey said, "I *believe* you. I swear to God I believe you. I don't think you're saying this just because we happen to be friends, on our way. I believe you, and more than anything else in the world I want to go to Ithaca with you. I want to live there and I want to do all the things you said." He stopped a moment to try to imagine what might go wrong to keep him from doing these things, and then he said, "If Bess doesn't like me—if she falls in love with somebody else—if she's married when we get there—I'm going to live in Ithaca anyway. I don't know, but Ithaca seems to be *my* home now, too. For the first time in my life I feel that I belong somewhere and—I hope you won't mind—I feel that my family is the Macauley family, because that's the kind of family I'd want for myself if I could choose. I hope to God Bess likes me or doesn't fall in love with someone else, because I *know* I like *her*." Now he spoke very softly, and even though the train was full of noise, Marcus could hear the words, "Even though Bess doesn't know it yet, she's mine. And from now on, every breath I take will be to keep me alive until I get to Ithaca and her. Ithaca's my home. That is where I live. That's where I want to be when I die—if I can."

237

"We'll get back," Marcus said. "We'll be in Ithaca some day, Bess and you and Mary and me, and my mother and Homer and Ulysses. You wait and see."

Now the two friends did not talk for a long time. They were greeted by other boys in the train and shouted with the others and even sang a song which these boys had themselves invented, a song about pin-up girls, their beauty, naming their favorites. And then in the midst of this song, as if what he was saying was altogether appropriate, Tobey said very simply, "Do you pray?" And Marcus replied, almost swiftly, "Always—always."

"At the orphanage," Tobey said, "we were *forced* to pray. It was a rule there. Whether we wanted to pray or not, we prayed."

"Maybe it's not such a bad rule," Marcus said, "but prayer is one thing you can't force. It's not a prayer if it's forced."

"I know," Tobey said. "That's why I quit praying when I left the orphanage. I don't think I've said a prayer since I was thirteen years old. But I'm starting all over again—right now—and this is it." He waited a moment and then, without closing his eyes, without bowing his head, without folding his hands, he began to pray, and what he said was unmistakably a prayer. "Just get me to Ithaca," he said, "if You can. Anything You say, but if You can, get me to Ithaca. Let me get home. Protect everybody. Keep everybody from pain. Find homes for the homeless. Get the traveler home and get me to Ithaca." He stopped and began singing again the words of their merry song. Suddenly he stopped singing and shouted, "Amen!"

"That's a good prayer," Marcus said. "I hope it's answered."

The orphan decided that he had left a few things out of the prayer. Therefore, he continued. "Keep the town there," he said. "Let me walk through its streets. Keep the Macauleys there—all of them. Keep Bess. Let her know I love her. Keep Marcus—and Mary. Keep his mother and his brother Homer and his brother Ulysses. Keep the house and the empty lot next door. Keep the harp and the piano and the songs. Keep the railroad tracks so I can see the trains go by. Keep the world where it is, and give me a chance to get to it—where I want to be—in Ithaca. Get me there—to Ithaca—if You can. That's all." And again he shouted, "Amen!"

Now the soldiers were singing another song which they had made up for themselves. This song had to do with the impermanence of all things, particularly a woman's love, and the boys delighted in the cynical wisdom of the song. Tobey and Marcus joined in the singing. Tobey stopped singing to say, "What do *you* pray for, Marcus?"

Marcus stopped singing to say, "I pray for the same things you pray for—the very same things." And again the two friends took up the song with the cynical wisdom.

After the song the whole train became silent. There was no reason for this silence and yet every man on the train was hushed and for a moment deeply solemn. At last a soldier named Joe Higgins came to Marcus and Tobey and said, "What's the matter, what's everybody so quiet about? How about a song, Tobey? How about playing for us on the accordion, Marcus?"

"What would you like to hear, Joe?" Marcus said.

"Oh, I don't know," Joe said. "We've sung all the rowdy songs, maybe we ought to sing something old —you know, something, well, something *good!* Why don't we sing a good old-time church song—something we all know and used to sing as kids?"

"Why not?" Marcus said. "What church song do you like, Joe?"

"Well," Joe said, "now don't you guys laugh at me—I'd sure like to hear *Leaning.* You know— *Leaning on the Everlasting Arms.*"

Marcus turned to Tobey. "Do you know the words of that song, Tobey?" he said. "If you don't, I can help you."

"Do I *know* them?" Tobey said. "I guess I sang that song almost every Sunday for ten years."

"All right," Marcus said, "let's do it for Joe." Marcus turned to Joe. "If you feel like joining in, Joe," he said, "you don't have to know how to sing. Just join in, that's all."

"Sure," Joe said, "I'm going to sing—sure."

Leaning on the Everlasting Arms

Marcus began to play the old hymn, and soon Tobey began to sing:

"What a fellowship, what a joy divine,
  Leaning on the everlasting arms;
  What a blessedness, what a peace is mine,
  Leaning on the everlasting arms."

Now in a strong, unmusical but nevertheless pleasant voice, Joe began to sing with Tobey, and soon everyone in the train was listening. After a moment everyone gathered around Marcus and Tobey and Joe to be nearer the music and the words of the wonderful old hymn. Joe and Tobey sang:

"Leaning, leaning, safe and secure from all alarms;
  Leaning, leaning, leaning on the everlasting arms."

By this time everybody gathered around the sing-ers was singing.

CHAPTER 32

A LETTER FROM MARCUS TO HIS BROTHER HOMER

This Saturday was one of the longest and most eventful days of Homer Macauley's life. Little things began to take on fresh importance and to mean something which he could understand. The sleep of last night, troubled and full of grief, was now forever a part of his wakefulness. He had tried with all his might to keep the messenger of Death from reaching Ithaca and its people. He had dreamed that, but now it was no longer a dream.

The letter from his brother Marcus was with him, unopened, waiting to be read.

A Letter from Marcus to Homer

He came into the telegraph office, limping, tired and eager to rest. He looked at the call sheet and there were no calls to take. He looked on the incoming telegram hook and there were no telegrams to deliver. His work was done. All was clear. He went to the old telegraph operator and said, "Mr. Grogan, would you like to chip in with me tonight for two day-old pies—apple and cocoanut cream?"

The old telegraph operator was by this time more than half drunk. "I'll chip in, boy," he said, "but I'll not have any of the pies—thanks just the same."

"If *you* don't want any of the pies, Mr. Grogan," Homer said, "I don't want any either. I thought *you* might be hungry. I'm not hungry at all. I haven't had a chance to take it easy all day until now. But I'm not hungry. It seems funny. You'd think a fellow would get hungry working all day and all night, but he doesn't. I had a bowl of chili at six tonight and that's all."

"How's your leg?" Grogan said.

"O.K.," Homer said. "I've forgotten all about it. I get around all right." He looked curiously at the old telegraph operator and then said very softly, "Are you drunk, Mr. Grogan?" He spoke earnestly and the old man was not offended or hurt.

"Yes, I am, boy," Mr. Grogan said. He went to his chair and sat down. After a moment he looked over at the boy across the table from him, not sitting but standing there. "I feel a lot better when I'm drunk," the old telegraph operator said. Then he brought the bottle out and took a good long drink. "I'm not going to tell you never to take a drink," he said. "I'm not going to say, as so many old fools do— *Learn a lesson from me. Look what drink did to me* —that would be a lot of nonsense. You're getting around now, seeing a lot of things—a lot of things you never saw before. Well, let me tell you something. Anything that concerns people—be very careful about it. If you see something you're sure is wrong, don't be sure. If it's people, be very careful. Now, you'll forgive me, but I must tell you, because you're a man I respect, so I don't mind trying to tell you that it's not right, it's foolish, to criticize the way any people happen to be. I haven't the slightest idea who you are—where you're from—how you came about—what made you the way you are—but I feel pleased about these things and I'm grateful. As a man gets closer to the end of his time he feels more and more grateful for the good people who're going to go on when he's gone. I might not be telling you this if I weren't drunk, so that alone is a good example of why it's wrong to have ideas about people who do things that everyone likes to feel aren't right. It's very important for me to tell you these things and for you to know them. Therefore, it is a good thing that I *am* drunk and that I am telling you. Can you understand what I'm saying?"

"I'm not sure, Mr. Grogan," Homer said.

"I'm telling you," the old telegraph operator said,

A Letter from Marcus to Homer

"something that may embarrass you. And I could not tell you unless I were drunk. I'm telling you this—be grateful for yourself. Yes, for *yourself*. Be thankful. Understand that what a man is is something he *can* be grateful for, and *ought* to be grateful for, because if he is good, his goodness is not his alone, it's mine too, and the other fellow's. It's his only to protect and to spread around for me and for everybody else in the world. What you have is good, so be thankful for it. It will be welcomed by everyone you meet at one time or another. They will know you the minute they see you."

Now for some reason Homer remembered the grief of the Mexican woman and the way she spoke to him, and as he remembered the old telegraph operator went on.

"They will know that you will not betray them or hurt them. They will know that you will not despise them after the whole world has despised them. They will know that you will see in them what the world has failed to see. You must know about that. You must not be embarrassed by it. You are a great man, fourteen years old. Who has made you great, nobody knows, but as it is true, know that it is true, be humble before it, and protect it. Do you understand?"

The messenger was extremely embarrassed, and it was very difficult for him to say, "I guess so, Mr. Grogan."

The old telegraph operator went on: "Then, I thank you. I have watched you, sober and drunk, since you came to work here, and, sober *or* drunk, I have recognized you. I have worked in cities in every part of the world. In my youth I wanted to reach many cities, and I reached them. All my life I have watched for you everywhere I have gone, and I have found you in many places—many out-of-the-way places—in many unknown people. I have found *something* of you in every man I have ever met, but most often it has not been enough. Now, in Ithaca, on my way home, I have found you again, better than ever, greater than ever. So, if you understand, I thank you. What is that you're holding—a letter? I have finished. Go ahead. Read your letter, boy."

"It's a letter from my brother Marcus," Homer said. "I haven't had a chance to open it yet."

"Then open it," the old telegraph operator said. "Read the letter from your brother. Read it aloud."

"Would you like to hear it, Mr. Grogan?" Homer said.

"Yes, if I may, I would like very much to hear it," the old telegraph operator said, and then took another drink.

Homer Macauley tore open the envelope of the letter from his brother Marcus, brought out the letter, unfolded it, and began to read, speaking very slowly.

"Dear Homer:" he read. "First of all, everything of mine at home is yours—to give to Ulysses when you no longer want them: my books, my phonograph, my records, my clothes when you're ready to fit into them, my bicycle, my microscope, my fishing tackle, my collection of rocks from Piedra, and all the other things of mine at home. They're yours rather than Bess's as you are now the man of the Macauley family of Ithaca. The money I made last year at the packing house I have given to Ma of course, to help out. It is not nearly enough, though, and soon Ma and Bess will be thinking of going to work. I cannot ask you not to allow them to go to work, but I am hoping that you yourself will not allow them to do so. I believe that you will not, as I know I would not. Ma would want to go to work, of course, and so would Bess. But that is all the more reason for you not to let them. I don't know how you are going to be able to keep our family together and go to high school at the same time, but I believe you will find a way. My Army pay goes to Ma, except for a few dollars that I must have, but this money is not enough. It is not easy for me to hope for so much from you, when I myself did not begin to work until I was nineteen, but somehow I believe that you will be able to do what I could not do.

"I miss you of course and I think of you all the time. I am happy, and even though I have never believed in wars—and know them to be foolish, even when they are necessary—I am proud that I am serving my country—which to me is Ithaca, our home, and all of the Macauleys. I do not recognize any enemy which is human, for no human being can be my enemy. Whoever he is, whatever color he is, however mistaken he may be in what he believes, he is my friend, not my enemy, for he is no different from myself. My quarrel is not with *him*, but with that in him which I seek to destroy in myself first.

"I do not feel like a hero. I have no talent for such feelings. I hate no one. I do not feel patriotic either, for I have always loved my country, its people, its towns, my home, and my family. I would rather I were not in the Army. I would rather there were no War, but as I *am* in the Army and as there *is* a War, I have long since made up my mind to be the best soldier it is possible for me to be. I have no idea what is ahead, but whatever it is I am humbly ready for it. I am terribly afraid—I must tell *you* this —but I know that when the time comes I shall do what is expected of me, and maybe even more than what is expected of me, but I want you to know I shall be obeying no command other than the command of my own heart. With me will be boys from all over America, from thousands of towns like Ithaca. I may be killed in this War. I must come right out and tell you this. I don't like the idea at all. More than anything else in the world I want to come back to Ithaca, and spend many long years with you and with my mother and sister and brother. I want to come back for Mary and a home and a family of my own. It is very likely that we shall be leaving soon—for action. Nobody knows where the action will be, but it is understood that we shall soon be leaving. Therefore, this may be my last letter to you for some time. I hope it is not the last of all. If it is, hold us together. Do not believe I am gone. Do not let the others believe it. My friend here is an orphan—a foundling—it is very strange that of all the boys here *he* should become my friend. His name is Tobey George. I have told him about Ithaca and our family. Some day I shall bring him to Ithaca with me. When you read this letter, do not be unhappy. I am glad that I am the Macauley who is in the War, for it would be a pity and a mistake if it were you.

"I can write to you what I could never say in words. You are the best of the Macauleys. You must go on being the best. Nothing must ever stop you. You are fourteen years old, but you must live to be twenty and then thirty and forty and fifty and sixty. You must live, in the years of your life, forever. I believe you will. I shall always be watching you. You are what we are fighting the War for. Yes, *you*—my brother. How could I ever tell you such things if we were together? You would jump on me and wrestle with me and call me a fool, but even so everything I have said is true. Now I will write your name here, to remind you: Homer Macauley. That's who you are. I miss you very much. I can't wait until I see you again. When that happens, when we meet again, I will let you wrestle me and put me down on my back in the parlor in front of Ma and

Bess and Ulysses and maybe Mary even—I'll let you do that because I will be so glad to see you again. God bless you. So long. Your brother, Marcus."

While he was reading the letter the messenger sat down. He read very slowly, gulping many times, and becoming sick many times as he had been sick first in the house of the Mexican mother and then the night that he had cried while riding his bicycle around Ithaca after work. Now he got up. His hands were trembling. He bit the corner of his lip and looked over at the old telegraph operator, who was as deeply moved by the letter as the messenger himself. He spoke very softly. "If my brother is killed in this stupid War," he said, "I shall spit at the world. I shall hate it forever. I won't be good. I shall be the worst of them all, the worst that ever lived."

He stopped suddenly and tears came to his eyes. He hurried to the locker behind the repeater rack, took off his uniform and got into his regular clothes. He was running out of the office almost before his clothes had been properly arranged.

The old telegraph operator sat a long time. It was very quiet when he shook himself at last, finished the rest of the bottle, got up and looked around the office.

CHAPTER 33

HERE IS A KISS

The pattern of life in Ithaca—of people everywhere in the world—followed a design which at first
seemed senseless and crazy, but as the days and
nights gathered together as months and years, the
pattern was seen to have had beauty of form. The
line of ugliness had been clothed in grace by the
line of charity. The force of brutality had been tem-
pered and sweetened by the greater force of gen-
tility. The evil color of wrong had been lost in the
bright color of right, and together they had become
a color more beautiful than the color of right alone.

Many times the telegraph box rattled and Mr.

Grogan sat at the typewriter and tapped out the messages of love and hope and pain and death from the world to its children. "I am coming home." "Don't worry." "The Department of War regrets to inform you that your son—" "Meet me at the Southern Pacific Depot." "Here is a kiss." "I am all right." "God bless you." Many times Homer Macauley delivered these messages.

In the parlor of the Macauley house the harp was plucked and the message of song was heard. The soldiers moved on, over land, over water, through the air, into new places, new days, new nights, new sleep, and new and strange moments filled with incredible noises, incredible problems and unbelievable and inhuman dangers. The faces of the living changed, but imperceptibly—Marcus, Tobey, Homer, Spangler, Grogan, Mrs. Macauley, Ulysses, Diana, Auggie, Lionel, Bess, Mary, John Strickman, three soldiers, Rosalie Simms-Peabody, Mr. Ara, his son John, Big Chris, Miss Hicks, and even Mr. Mechano.

The freight train with the Negro leaning over the side of the gondola moved on. The gopher peeked out of the earth. The apricots of Mr. Henderson's tree took on the smiling color of the sun and the freckles of the boys who came to steal them. The brooding hen came forth with her nation of chicks. Ulysses watched. The limp in Homer's leg healed. Easter Sunday came to Ithaca. And then the Sunday after Easter. And then another Sunday, and then another, and then another and another.

All of the Macauleys of Ithaca sat with Mary Arena on *this* Sunday in the First Ithaca Presbyterian Church. Ulysses sat on the aisle. Directly in front of him, by strange accident, sat a man with a bald head. This object was fascinating to behold: the shape alone was something to study, being not unlike the shape of the egg. The half dozen hairs of the bald head, growing in a lonely group, were unashamed and heroic. The wrinkle which divided the head as the equator divides the earth was a miracle of design. The whole head was magnificent to Ulysses.

Now Reverend Holly and the congregation were engaged in a pious oral duel—on the theme of the Blessed Life. First Reverend Holly read a verse, then the congregation answered in one powerful and tender voice.

"And seeing the multitudes," Reverend Holly chanted, "He went up into a mountain, and when He was seated, His disciples came unto Him.

"And He opened His mouth," the congregation replied, *"and taught them, saying:*

"Blessed are the poor: for theirs is the kingdom of heaven.

"Blessed are they that mourn: for they shall be comforted.

"Blessed are the meek: for they shall inherit the earth.

"Blessed are they which do hunger and thirst after righteousness: for they shall be filled.

"Blessed are the merciful: for they shall obtain mercy.

"Blessed are the pure in heart: for they shall see God.

"Blessed are the peacemakers: for they shall be called the children of God.

"Rejoice, and be exceeding glad: Ye are the salt of the earth. Ye are the light of the world.

"Let your light so shine before men that they may see your good works and glorify your Father which is in heaven."

The responsive reading from the Scriptures began while Ulysses Macauley was studying the bald head. Suddenly this object was decorated by a fly which began to explore the bald head and to brighten the half-asleep spirit of the little boy. Ulysses watched the fly a moment and then slowly reached out to catch it, but Mrs. Macauley took his hand gently and held it. Staring steadily at the bald head and the fly, thinking of nothing in particular, and then falling away into a daydream, Ulysses now saw the smooth skin of the bald head as a desert. He saw the wrinkle across the head as a stream, the group of seven hairs as palm trees, and the fly as a lion. Then he saw himself, in his Sunday clothes, on one side of the stream, with the lion on the other. Ulysses stood on the bank of the stream looking across at the lion, which in turn came directly opposite Ulysses to look at *him*. The Scripture reading continued.

In the distance Ulysses saw an Arab, in flowing robes, lying asleep upon the sand. Beside the Arab was a mandolin, or some such musical instrument, and a pitcher of water. Ulysses saw the lion, in a peace and innocence not unlike the sleeping man's, move to the man's head and bend down to smell him, but surely not to harm him.

The Scripture reading ended. The church organ breathed mightily, and the choir and the congregation began to sing *Rock of Ages*.

The vision of the desert vanished from the little boy's dream. In its place appeared an ocean. Clinging to a rock which rose several feet above the surface of this desolation of water was Ulysses himself. Only his head and hands were above water. He looked around for escape or rescue, but all that he could see was water. Even so, he was patient and full of faith. At last, far in the distance, walking on the water, Ulysses saw the great man, Big Chris. Big Chris came to Ulysses and without a word reached down to him, took him by the hand and lifted him out of the water onto the surface of it. After a moment, however, Ulysses fell back into the water, splashing, and once again Big Chris fished him out and set him on his feet. Holding the boy's hand, Big Chris went walking upon the water with Ulysses. Far away, the towers of a beautiful white city became visible and around the city, earth and vegetation. The man and the boy walked toward the city.

The song ended. Suddenly somebody was shaking Ulysses. He woke with a start. It was Lionel who was shaking him, Lionel—with a collection plate. Ulysses found his nickel, placed it in the plate, and passed the plate to his mother.

Lionel whispered to Ulysses, speaking piously and with an air of great mystery. "Are you saved, Ulysses?" he said.

"What?" Ulysses said.

"Read this," Lionel said, and handed his friend a religious pamphlet.

Ulysses studied the pamphlet, but could not read the very big letters which formed these words: "Are you saved? It is never too late."

On the other side of the aisle Lionel asked an elderly gentleman the same question. "Are you saved?" he said.

The man looked at the boy severely and then whispered impatiently, "Go along, boy."

Before going, however, and somewhat in the manner of a martyr, Lionel offered the elderly gentleman one of the pamphlets. The elderly gentleman, irritated, quietly slapped the pamphlet out of Lionel's hands, scaring the boy and making him feel like one of the greater martyrs.

The elderly gentleman's wife whispered to him, "What is it, dear?"

"The boy asked me if I was saved," the elderly

gentleman said. "Then he handed me *this*." The man reached down and picked the pamphlet off the floor and handed it to his wife. "He handed me this —this *pamphlet!*" The elderly gentleman read the words with some irritation. "Are you saved? It is never too late."

The wife patted the hand of the elderly gentleman and said, "It's nothing. How should the boy know that you've been a missionary in China for thirty years?"

All during the ritual of taking collection, the organ played softly and sweetly and a soprano sang. Lionel, Auggie, Shag and a number of the other boys of Ithaca stood at the back of the center aisle, each holding a collection plate, until the music ended. Then in a wondrous and comic silence and seriousness the boys stamped down the aisle to the table directly beneath the pulpit, where they put the collection plates, one on top of the other, and then took their places beside their parents.

CHAPTER 34

THE LAUGHTER OF THE LION

After church and Sunday dinner, August Gottlieb was in his front yard patching an old tennis net into something which he hoped might turn out to be useful. Enoch Hopper, a boy of Auggie's age, came by swiftly, stopped swiftly, and watched swiftly. He was the owner of an old baseball with the cover gone, which he slammed onto the sidewalk fiercely, making it bounce very high. He caught the ball and slammed it again and again. Enoch Hopper was the most high-strung boy in Ithaca, the most restless, the swiftest-moving, the most impatient, and the loudest-talking.

"What are you making, Auggie?" he said.

"Net," Auggie said.

"What for?" Enoch said. "Fish?"

"No," Auggie said, "animals."

Already Enoch Hopper was bored. "Come on," he said, "let's start a baseball game or go out to Guggenheim's water tank and climb it."

"Got to fix the net," Auggie said.

"Ah, what've you got to fix the net for?" Enoch shouted impatiently.

"Catch animals," Auggie said.

"Where do you see any animals around here?" the high-strung boy said. "Come on, let's go," he shouted. "Let's go out to Malaga and go swimming."

"I'll catch animals in this net all right," Auggie said.

"Couldn't catch a flea with that tennis net," Enoch Hopper said. "Come on, let's start a game. Let's go down and sneak into the Bijou, see a Tarzan picture."

"I'll catch a dog first," Auggie said, "just to test the net—just to see if it works. And then if it *does* work, watch out!"

"Ah, that's an old tennis net," Enoch said. "You won't catch anything with it. Let's go down to the courthouse park, to the city jail and talk to the prisoners."

"I've got to fix my animal net," Auggie said. "I'm going to try it out today—and if it works—oh, boy—tomorrow!"

"Oh, boy, *what?*" Enoch said. "There's no animals around here. A cow. A couple of dogs. Six or seven rabbits. A few chickens—what are you going to catch?"

"I got a good net here," Auggie said. "Big enough for a bear."

"Ah, come on, let's go," Enoch said. "What do you want to be fooling with an old tennis net for? Big enough for a bear? You couldn't catch a teddy-bear with that net. Let's go down to Chinatown and walk down China Alley."

August Gottlieb interrupted his work a moment to think about Chinatown and the Chinese. He looked up at Enoch Hopper and said, "You afraid of the Chinese?"

"Naaah," Enoch said truthfully. "I ain't afraid of nothing. Even if they were dangerous they couldn't catch *me*. Too fast. Too fast on my feet."

"I bet a lion couldn't catch you," Auggie said.

"Naaah," Enoch said, "I'm too fast. A lion couldn't get anywhere near me. Bears, tigers, Chinese—anybody. I'm too fast for them. Come on, let's go over across the Southern Pacific tracks and get into a game with the Cosmos Playground gang."

"I'll bet you'd be *harder* to catch in a trap than a lion," Auggie said.

"No trap in the world fast enough to catch me," Enoch said. "Let's go out to the fair grounds and run around the mile track. I'll give you a hundred yards head start."

"I'll bet your own father couldn't catch you," Auggie said.

"Naaah," Enoch said, "couldn't come anywhere near me. I'd leave him in the dust."

Now Lionel came up. "What are you making, Auggie?" he said.

"Net," Auggie said—"to catch animals."

"Couldn't catch a flea with that net, Lionel," Enoch said. "Come on, let's go out on the empty lot and play catch. How about it?"

"*Me?*" Lionel said.

"Sure, Lionel," Enoch said. "Come on. You throw 'em to me real hard. I'll throw 'em to you real easy. Come on, come on, half the afternoon's gone."

"All right, Enoch," Lionel said, "but remember—throw 'em easy. I ain't so good at catch. Sometimes I miss and the ball hits me in the face. Hurt my eyes once, my nose twice."

"I'll throw 'em easy. Don't worry," Enoch said. "Come on, come on."

Enoch Hopper and Lionel Cabot moved across the street to the empty lot and Auggie went back to his work. Soon he had all of the pieces of the old tennis net sewn together, so that there was an almost square piece of netting. He stretched this netting out and attached each corner to a stick in the ground so that he could behold what he had made. Now Shag Manoogian came over the back yard fence to Auggie. "What's that?" he said.

"Net," Auggie said—"to catch animals. Want to help me try it out?"

"Sure," Shag said. "How are you going to do it?"

"Well," Auggie said, "I'll hold the net and hide here behind Ara's store. You call Enoch. He's over there playing catch with Lionel. Enoch is swifter and harder to catch than a lion. If this net can hold Enoch, it can hold anything. All right. I'm hiding. I'm ready. Call Enoch. Tell him you want to ask him something."

"O.K.," Shag said. He looked over at Enoch on the empty lot and then called out very loud, "Enoch! Oh, Enoch!"

Enoch Hopper turned and shouted back, twice as loud, "What do you want, Shag?"

"Come here, Enoch," Shag shouted. "I want to ask you something."

"What do you want to ask me?" Enoch shouted.

"I'll tell you when you get here," Shag shouted.

"O.K.," Enoch shouted, and started running toward Shag, with Lionel following but not quite sure whether he should run or walk.

"All right, Shag," Auggie whispered. "Duck back here and hide with me. Take hold of this end of the net. When he comes around the corner of the store we'll jump on him and capture him. See?"

Running swiftly, Enoch shouted, "Let's go out to Malaga and go swimming. Half the afternoon's gone already. Let's do something. What are we waiting for?"

The Laughter of the Lion

Enoch came running around the corner of Mr. Ara's market. Auggie and Shag leaped out swiftly and spread the net over him. Sure enough, Enoch Hopper moved like a wild undomesticated animal, perhaps a lion. The two big-game hunters worked furiously but the net was not quite strong enough, and soon Enoch Hopper was standing upright, completely unoffended and very much interested in the outcome of the test.

He slammed the baseball on the sidewalk. "Come on, Auggie," he shouted, "let's go! That net couldn't catch a flea! Come on! What are we waiting for?"

"O.K.," Auggie said, and threw the net into the yard. "Let's go to the courthouse park and talk to the prisoners."

Auggie, Enoch, Shag, and, not far behind them, Lionel moved on down the street toward the courthouse park. Soon Enoch Hopper was a block ahead of the others, shouting back at them, "Come on! Hurry up! What are you moving so slow for?" He threw the baseball at a bird which had come down in a tree, but missed it.

CHAPTER 35

THE TREES AND THE VINES

Thomas Spangler and Diana Steed were in the country for a Sunday afternoon drive around Kingsburg. The car was an old roadster with the top down.

"Those," he said, pointing to a row of trees bordering a vineyard, "are fig trees. The vines beyond them are Muscat vines. There's some olive trees. That tree's a pomegranate. Those vines over there are Malaga vines. There's an orchard of peach trees. These are apricots. This valley is the most beautiful valley in the world. There's a walnut tree. There's a tree you don't see very often—persimmon. Everything wonderful grows in this valley."

"Oh, darling," the young woman said, "you do love trees, don't you?"

"I love everything," Spangler said, and then added swiftly, "Now don't ask me if I love *you*, because I do. I love you, and I love the whole world, and everything in it." He lifted his voice, almost shouting. "And I saw a pure river of life, clear as crystal. In the midst of the street of it and on either side of the river was the tree of life which bare twelve manner of fruits, and the leaves of the tree were for the healing of nations." Spangler kissed the corner of the young woman's eye.

"Oh, darling," she said, "are you happy?"

"Sure, sure," Spangler said swiftly. "I don't go much for that happiness stuff, but whatever happiness may be, I've got a pretty good idea it's something like this. There's some more olive trees."

He put his arm around the young woman and said, "You must know I can't wait to see who it is. I think I'd like it to be a little girl. I think I'd like to have a little girl around looking like you. I think I'd like to hear the voice of a little girl like that." He went on gently. "I used to think you were a fool." Now he kissed the young woman on the mouth. "Well, anybody who can do *that* is no fool. And you *can* do it."

"Oh, I want to, darling," the young woman said.

"and I'm not the least bit afraid. Not the least bit."

The little automobile moved along parallel with Kings River near the picnic grounds. On this Sunday afternoon five big picnics were going on—with music and dancing—Italians, Greeks, Croats and Serbs, Armenians, and Americans. Each group had its own kind of music and dancing. Spangler stopped the automobile at each group for a minute or two in order to be able to listen to the singing and to watch the dancing. He had something to say about each group. "Those are Greeks over there," he said. "I can tell from the music. I used to know a family of Greeks. See the girl dancing? That's the way they dance in the old country."

The car moved on a short distance and stopped again. "Those people over there are the Armenians," he said. "I can tell from the priests and the kids. That's what they believe in—God and lots of children. They're something like the Greeks. And something like everybody else. See the old man dancing? Listen to that music." The car moved on and again it stopped before another group. "I think those people are Croats and Serbs," Spangler said, "and maybe a few other people from around in there. They're all the same."

He put his arm around the young woman and said to her swiftly, "I think I'd like it to be a little Serbian girl—but maybe she could have a little Greek in her, too. Or a little Armenian or Italian or Polish or Russian, maybe. I'd like it to have some

German and Spanish and French, too—a little of everything."

The car moved and then stopped again. "You know who those are," Spangler said to the young woman. "The Italians. Corbett himself is probably out there somewhere with his wife and kids. Hear them singing? *O Sole Mio.*"

The automobile moved to the last group of picnickers. This group was perhaps the most wonderful of them all. It was the *wildest,* surely. The music was swing, jive and boogie-woogie, and the dancing was terrific. "Americans!" Spangler said. "Look at them. Americans—Greeks, Serbs, Poles, Russians, Armenians, Germans, Spaniards, Portuguese, Italians, Abyssinians, Jews, French, English, Scotch, Irish—look at them! Listen to them!"

They looked and listened and then after a moment the automobile moved away.

CHAPTER 36

ITHACA, MY ITHACA!

The afternoon Santa Fé passenger train from San Francisco stopped at Ithaca and nine people got off, among them two young soldiers. But before the train moved on, a third soldier, with a limp in his left leg, got off and walked away, moving very slowly.

The first soldier looked at his friend and said, "Well, brother, this is Ithaca. This is home."

"Boy, let me look at it," the second soldier said. "Just let me look at it." Now he hummed the delight he felt. "Ummmmmmmm-man! My home, Ithaca! I don't know how *you* feel, but *this* is how I feel." The soldier got down on his knees and kissed the brick of the depot floor. "A kiss for my Ithaca," he said. And then he kissed it again. "Another kiss," he said. And then he kissed it again and said, "Another."

"Come on, Henry," the first soldier said. "Get up. People are looking. You want them to think soldiers are crazy?"

"No, I don't," Henry said, "but I can't help it. Boy, my Ithaca!" He got up and took his friend by the arm. "Come on, Danny, let's go," he said.

"You think your folks are going to be surprised to see *you?*" Danny said. "Well, wait until my folks see *me*. They're going to be so surprised they aren't going to be able to see straight."

The two boys came up the block together. It was the street where Mr. Ara had his market. Suddenly they began to run, one boy running up onto the porch of one house and the other up onto the porch of the house next door. Alf Rife came running around one house and stood on the front lawn between the two houses, watching. The front door of each house opened at the same time. The women who opened the doors embraced the boys at the same time. And now men and boys and girls and women all joined in together embracing the soldiers. But there seemed to be a mistake. Alf Rife discovered the mistake and began shouting at the top of his voice.

"Wrong boy," he shouted, "wrong boy! It's Danny Booth, the neighbor's boy! He's come home.

He lives next door. Came to the wrong house. We thought it was *our* boy. It's Mrs. Booth's boy. There's our boy over there kissing Mrs. Booth. Wrong boy, Ma, wrong boy!"

"Oh, hello, Danny," Mrs. Rife said to Danny Booth. "We thought you was Henry."

"Oh, that's all right, Mrs. Rife," Danny said. "I'll go over and kiss Ma, too. You come over, too."

On the porch of the other house Henry Rife said, "Hello, Mrs. Booth. Come on over to our house, *all* of you. It sure is good to see you, Mrs. Booth." He kissed her again. "Danny's over on my porch kissing my mother."

Now the lawns of the two yards filled with people going and coming in a kind of delightful confusion, with the boy Alf Rife shouting over and over again, "Wrong boy, wrong boy! He came to the wrong house! He lives next door. Hey, Henry—*here's* Ma! That's Mrs. Booth! Wrong house, Henry!"

CHAPTER 37

LOVE IS IMMORTAL, HATE DIES EVERY MINUTE

Homer Macauley, his sister Bess, his brother Ulysses and their friend Mary Arena taking a Sunday afternoon walk through Ithaca, passed the line of people standing in front of the Kinema Theatre and among them discovered Lionel. Homer stopped.

"Hello, Lionel," he said. "Going to see a movie?"

"Haven't got any money," Lionel said.

"Then what are you standing in line for?" Homer said.

"Me and Auggie and Shag and Enoch," Lionel said, "we came to the courthouse park to talk to the criminals. Then they chased me away. I didn't know where to go. I saw these people standing here, so I came and stood with them."

"How long have you been standing here?" Homer said.

"An hour, I guess," Lionel said.

"Well," Homer said, "do you *want* to see the movie?" He brought some money out of his pocket.

"I don't know," Lionel said. "I didn't have any place to go. I don't like movies very much."

"Well," Homer said, "come on with us. We're only taking a walk, window-shopping. We'll walk around town awhile and then go home. Come on with us, Lionel." He lifted the rope and Lionel got out of the line.

"Thanks," Lionel said. "I sure was getting tired standing there that way."

As they walked, Ulysses stopped suddenly and tugged at Homer's hand. He pointed down at the sidewalk. There before the boy was a Lincoln penny, face up.

"A penny!" Homer said. "Pick it up, Ulysses, it's good luck. Keep it—always!"

Ulysses picked up the penny and looked around at everybody, smiling at his good luck.

They passed the telegraph office from across the street and Homer stopped to look over at the little office.

"That's where I work," he said. "That's where

272

I've worked almost six months now." He stopped a moment and then, as if talking to himself, he said, "It seems more like a hundred years." Homer looked into the office and then he said, "I think that's Mr. Grogan. I didn't know Mr. Grogan was working today." He turned to the others. "Wait here a minute, will you?" he said. "I'll be right back."

He crossed the street and hurried into the office. The telegraph box in front of Mr. Grogan was rattling, but the old telegraph operator was not taking down the telegram that was being dispatched. Homer ran up to him and said, "Mr. Grogan, Mr. Grogan!" But the old man did not wake up.

The messenger ran out of the office and across the street to the others. "Mr. Grogan's not feeling good," he said. "I've got to go back and take care of him. You go along home. I'll be home after a while."

"All right, Homer," Bess said.

"What's the matter with him?" Lionel said, not even knowing who it was he was talking about.

"I've got to hurry back," Homer said. "Now go along. He's an old man, Lionel, that's all."

Homer hurried back to the telegraph office and shook Mr. Grogan several times. He ran over to the water jar and filled a paper cup, then splashed the water into the face of the old man. Mr. Grogan opened his eyes. "It's me, Mr. Grogan," Homer said. "I didn't know you were working today or I would have come down long ago, like I always do when you work on Sundays. I was just passing by. I'll hurry and get the coffee."

The old telegraph operator shook his head, reached out to the telegraph key and interrupted the telegrapher at the other end. He put a telegram blank into the typewriter and began to type a message.

Homer ran out of the office to Corbett's on the corner and asked for coffee.

"He's making fresh coffee now, Homer," Pete, the waiter, said. "Be a minute or two."

"Hasn't he got any cooked?" Homer said.

"Fresh out," Pete said. "He's cooking a new pot now."

"It's very important," Homer said. "I'll go back to the office a minute and then I'll come back here. Maybe by that time the coffee will be ready."

When Homer got back to Mr. Grogan, the old telegraph operator was not typing the telegram that was coming over the wire. Again Homer shook him. "Mr. Grogan," he said, "they're sending a telegram! You're not getting it! Stop them, Mr. Grogan! Tell them to wait a minute. They're making fresh coffee at Corbett's. I'll have a cup here for you in a minute or two. Stop them, Mr. Grogan! You're not getting the telegram."

Homer turned and ran out of the office.

The old telegraph operator looked at the telegram he had been typing. He read over what he had typed so far:

Love Is Immortal

MRS. KATE MACAULEY
2226 SANTA CLARA AVENUE
ITHACA, CALIFORNIA
THE DEPARTMENT OF WAR REGRETS TO INFORM YOU
THAT YOUR SON MARCUS . . .

The old telegraph operator tried to get up from his chair, but now the attack came again and he clutched at his heart. After a moment he fell forward to rest upon the typewriter.

Homer Macauley came walking into the telegraph office with a cup of coffee rattling in his hand. He came up to the old man and set the cup down on the table. Now the telegraph box stopped its rattling and the whole office became very quiet.

"Mr. Grogan!" Homer said. "What's the matter?" He moved the old man back, away from the typewriter, to look into his face, and as he did so, he noticed the incomplete telegram in the typewriter. Without even reading the words of the telegram, Homer knew the message, and yet refused to believe it. He stood as if paralyzed, holding the old man. "Mr. Grogan!" he said.

Felix, the Sunday messenger, came in and looked over at the old man and at the messenger. "What's the matter, Homer?" he said. "What's wrong with the old man?"

"He's dead," Homer said.

"Ah, you're crazy," Felix said.

"No," Homer said. He spoke almost furiously. "He's dead."

"I'll call Mr. Spangler," Felix said. He dialed a number on the telephone, waited, and then hung up. "He's not home," Felix said. "What'll we do?" He came over to see what it was that Homer was staring at in the typewriter. After reading the telegram, Felix said, "It's not finished, Homer. Maybe your brother is only hurt or missing."

Homer looked at Mr. Grogan and then said, "No, *he* heard the rest of the telegram. He didn't type it out, but he *heard* it."

"Maybe he didn't," Felix said. "I'll telephone Mr. Spangler again. Maybe he's home now."

Homer Macauley looked around the telegraph office. Suddenly he spat with terrible fury and contempt. He sat down and looked straight before him. There were no tears in his eyes.

Thomas Spangler drew up in his automobile in front of the telegraph office after the drive in the country. He sounded the horn and Felix ran out to the automobile.

"Mr. Spangler," Felix said, "I've been trying to get you on the telephone. Something's happened! It's Mr. Grogan! Homer says he's dead!"

"You go on home," Spangler said to Diana Steed. "I'll be around later—but don't expect me for supper. Maybe you'd better go out and spend the night with your folks." He got out of the car and kissed the young woman.

"All right, darling," she said.

Spangler hurried into the telegraph office. He

looked at Mr. Grogan and then at Homer. He turned to the other messenger. "Felix," he said, "telephone Dr. Nelson—1133. Tell him to come right down."

Spangler lifted the old man out of the chair and carried him to the couch at the back of the telegraph office. He came back and looked at Homer Macauley. "Don't feel bad, Homer," he said. "Mr. Grogan was an old man. This is the way he wanted it to be. Come on, now, don't feel bad."

Now the telegraph box rattled and Spangler went to answer the call. When he sat down in Mr. Grogan's chair he saw the unfinished telegram. He looked at it a long time and then he looked across the table at Homer. Spangler telegraphed the operator at the other end, asking questions about the unfinished telegram. The telegrapher at the other end tapped out the full message again. Spangler telegraphed the other operator to postpone any more telegrams for a while. He then got up and went to his desk and sat down, looking at nothing. His hand fell idly on the hard-boiled egg which he kept for good luck. Without knowing what he was doing, he tapped the egg idly on the desk until the shell broke and then slowly he removed all the shell, and in a kind of desperate stupor, ate the egg. Suddenly he discovered the shell of the egg on the table and pushed it off into the wastebasket.

"Felix," he said, "call Harry Burke, the telegraph

operator, and tell him to come right down. When the doctor comes, tell him to take care of everything. I'll talk to him later."

Homer Macauley got up, went to the typewriter and took the unfinished telegram out of it. He filed the carbon copy of the unfinished telegram in its proper place, folded the original and put it in an envelope. He put the envelope in his coat pocket. Spangler went to the messenger and put his arm around him. "Come on, Homer," he said, "let's go for a walk."

They left the telegraph office and walked two blocks in silence. At last Homer began to speak. "What's a man supposed to do?" he said very calmly, almost gently. "I don't know who to hate. I keep trying to find out who it is, but I *can't* find out who it is. I just don't know. What's a man going to do? What can I do about it? What can I say? How does a man go on living? Who does he love?"

Now, coming down the street toward them, Homer and Spangler saw Auggie, Enoch, Shag, and Nickie. The boys greeted Homer and he greeted each of them by name. It was almost evening now. The sun was going down, the sky was red, and the city was darkening.

"Who can you hate?" Homer said. "I don't know anybody to hate. Byfield knocked me down when I was running the low hurdles, but I can't hate *him*, even. That's just the way he happens to be. I don't know what it is. I don't know who does it. I can't figure it out at all. The only thing I want to know is, What about my brother? That's all I want to know. Nothing like this has ever happened to me before. When my father died it was different. He had lived a good life. He had raised a good family. We were sad because he was dead, but we weren't sore. Now I'm sore and I haven't got anybody to be sore at. Who's the enemy? Do you know, Mr. Spangler?"

It was some time before the manager of the telegraph office could answer the messenger. "I know the enemy isn't people," he said. "If it were, then I would be my own enemy. The people of the world are like one man. If they hate one another, it is themselves they hate. A man cannot hate others— it is always himself. And if a man hates himself, there is only one thing for him to do—and that's leave—leave his body, leave the world, leave the people of the world. Your brother didn't want to leave, he wanted to stay. He *will* stay."

"How?" Homer said. "How will he stay?"

"I don't know how," Spangler said, "but I *have* to believe that he will stay. Maybe he will stay in you, in your little brother Ulysses. Maybe he will stay in the love you have for him."

"No," Homer said. "No, that isn't enough. I want to *see* him. I can't help it, but I want to see him the same way Ulysses wants to see him. I want to see him walking and standing. I want to smell him. I

279

want to talk to him. I want to hear his voice. I want to hear him laughing. I want to have fights with him even—the way we used to. Now, where will I find him? If I look everywhere I won't find him. The whole world is different now. All the people in the world are different now. Something good has gone out of them. Everything in Ithaca is changed now because my brother is not going to look at anything any more."

Now they were walking through the courthouse park, past the city jail, over to the games.

"I'm not going to try to comfort you," Spangler said. "I know I couldn't. But try to remember that a good man can never die. You will see him many times. You will see him in the streets. You will see him in the houses, in all the places of the town. In the vineyards and orchards, in the rivers and clouds, in all the things here that make this a world for us to live in. You will feel him in all things that are here out of love, and *for* love—all the things that are abundant, all the things that grow. The person of a man may leave—or be taken away—but the best part of a good man stays. It stays forever. Love is immortal and makes all things immortal. But hate dies every minute. Are you any good at pitching horseshoes?"

"No, sir," Homer said. "Not very."

"Neither am I," Spangler said. "Would you care to pitch a game of horseshoes before it's too dark?"

"Yes, sir," Homer said.

CHAPTER 38

THE END AND THE
BEGINNING

The limping soldier who got off the train which brought Danny Booth and Henry Rife home to Ithaca, began to walk around the town. He walked slowly, looking at everything, and talking to himself.

"This is Ithaca!" he said. "There's the depot—the Santa Fé—and there's the Ithaca sky over it. There's the Kinema Theatre, with the wonderful people of Ithaca standing in line. This is the Public Library. There's the Presbyterian Church. There's Ithaca High School, and this is the athletic field. There's Santa Clara Avenue and Ara's Market, and there's the house! There it is. There's my home!"

The soldier stood staring at the house a long time. "Ma and Bess," he said, "Homer and Ulysses. Mary next door, and her father, Mr. Arena." No thought said what was now said, only blood. "Ithaca, oh, Ithaca!" The soldier moved on. "There's the court-house park," he said. "Here's the city jail with the prisoners at the windows. And there are a couple of Ithaca men pitching a game of horseshoes." The soldier walked slowly toward the two men and leaned against the wire fence.

Homer Macauley and Thomas Spangler pitched horseshoes in silence, not even counting points. It was too dark now for the game, but they went on pitching. Homer started when he noticed the soldier leaning against the fence. For some reason it seemed to him that he knew this soldier. He moved toward the young man, looking into his face.

"Excuse me for staring," he said. "I thought I knew you."

"That's all right," the soldier said.

"Would you care to *pitch* a game?" Homer said. "You can take my place. It's a little dark, of course."

"No, thanks," the soldier said, "you go ahead. I'll just watch."

"I don't think I've ever seen you before," Homer said. "Is Ithaca your home?"

"Yes, it is," the soldier said. "I've come back—to stay."

"You mean," Homer said, "you don't have to go back to the War?"

282

The End and the Beginning

"No," the soldier said, "they've sent me home—for good. I got off the train a couple of hours ago. I've been walking around the town, looking at everything again."

"Well, why don't you go home?" Homer said. "Don't you want your family to know you're here?"

"I'll go home," the soldier said. "Of course I want my family to know I'm here. I'll go home little by little. I want to see as much as I can, first. I can't see enough of it. I can't believe I'm here. I'll walk around some more and then I'll go home."

The soldier went off slowly, limping. Homer Macauley stared after him, wondering.

"I don't know," he said to Spangler, "I seem to think I know that fellow. I don't feel like pitching any more, Mr. Spangler," he said. And then after a moment he said, "What shall I do? What am I going to tell them? They're waiting for me at home now. I know they are. I told them I'd be home for supper. How am I going to go into the house and look at them? They'll know everything the minute they see me. I don't *want* to tell them, but I know they'll know."

Spangler put his arm around Homer. "Wait," he said. "Don't go home just yet. Sit down here. Wait awhile. It takes a little time."

They sat quietly on a park bench, not talking. After a while Homer said, "What am I waiting for?"

"Well," Spangler said, "you're waiting for the part of *him* that died to die in you, too—the part

283

that's only flesh—the part that comes and goes. That dying is hurting you now, but wait awhile. When the pain becomes death and leaves you, the rest will be lighter and better than ever. It takes a little time, and as long as you live it will take a little time, again and again, but each time it goes it will leave you closer than ever to the best that is in all men. Be patient with it, you will go home at last with no death in you. Give it time to go. I'll sit with you here until it's gone."

"Yes, sir," Homer said. The manager of the telegraph office and the messenger sat in the courthouse park of Ithaca, waiting.

Now the strings of the harp in the Macauley house soothed the pain out of all things. The face of the one who plucked the strings of the harp was a face radiant and strong and full of love. The girl who played the piano was one whose heart was earnest and innocent, and the girl who sang was one whose spirit was gentle and sweet. The small boy listening listened with the ears of all the living and watched with eyes full of faith in all things. The young man sitting on the steps of the front porch, the soldier, the boy who had come home to a town he had never before seen, to a house he had never before entered, to a family he had never known—was everybody. And he *was* home. Ithaca *was* the place of his birth. The house *was* the house he grew up in. The family inside the house *was* his family.

The End and the Beginning

Suddenly Ulysses Macauley was standing at the open front door, pointing. His sister Bess went over to see what it was. She turned to her mother. "Ma," she said, "somebody's sitting on our front-porch steps."

"Well," Mrs. Macauley said, "go on out to him, Bess, and ask him in—whoever he is. You needn't be afraid."

Bess Macauley went out onto the porch. "Won't you come in?" she said to the soldier. "My mother would like you to come in."

The soldier turned slowly and looked up at the girl. He spoke very quietly. "Bess," he said. "Sit down beside me! Sit down beside me until I am quiet inside and able to stand again. My legs are trembling, and if I try to stand now, I'll fall. Sit beside me, Bess."

The girl sat down on the steps beside the young man. "How do you know my name?" she said softly. "Who are you?"

"I don't know who I am," the soldier said, "but I know who *you* are, and who your mother is, and who your brothers are. Sit close to me, Bess—until I quiet down."

"Do you know my brother Marcus?" Bess said.

"Yes," the soldier said. "Your brother gave me my life—a place of birth—a family. Yes, I know him—he is *my* brother, too."

"Where is Marcus?" Bess said. "Why hasn't he come home with you?"

"Bess," the soldier said. He handed the girl a ring Marcus Macauley had given him. "Your brother Marcus sent you this."

Bess Macauley did not speak for some time and then she said, "Is Marcus dead?" Her voice was hushed, not excited.

"No," the soldier said. "Bess, believe me." He kissed the girl on the mouth. "He is not dead."

Homer Macauley came walking down the street. His sister Bess ran out to him. "Homer!" she said. "He's come from Marcus. They were friends. He's sitting on our steps." She turned and ran into the house.

Homer Macauley stood looking at Tobey George. "Tobey?" he said. "I thought I knew you when we talked in the park." He waited a moment and then said. "The telegram came this afternoon. I have it in my pocket. What are we going to do?"

"Tear it up, Homer," the soldier said. "Throw it away. It's not true, tear it up."

Homer brought the telegram out of his pocket and swiftly tore it up. He put the small pieces back into his pocket—to keep, forever.

"Please help me up," the soldier said. "We'll go into the house together." Homer Macauley leaned down to Tobey George, the orphan who had come home at last, and the soldier took the messenger by the shoulders and slowly got to his feet.

Now Homer lifted his voice. There was no sadness in his words or in his way of saying them.

The End and the Beginning

"Ma!" he said. "Bess! Mary! play some music. The soldier's come home! Welcome him!"

The music began.

"Let me stand here a moment and listen," the soldier said.

Homer Macauley and Tobey George listened to the music, each of them smiling, the soldier with a tender painfulness and the messenger with a kind of happiness he could not yet understand.

Mary Arena began to sing now, and then Ulysses Macauley came out of the house and took the hand of the soldier. When the song ended, Mrs. Macauley and Bess and Mary came to the open door. The mother, standing, looking at her two remaining sons, one on each side of the stranger, the soldier who had known her son who was now dead, smiled and understood. She smiled at the *soldier*. Her smile was for him who was now himself her son. She smiled as if he were Marcus himself and the soldier and his two brothers moved toward the door, toward the warmth and light of home.

For Reflection, Conversation, Writing, and Sketching

The noble and ridiculous world and its constant comedy

Most people read right through *The Human Comedy* without stopping; one reader did so in an hour and a half. After reading it, you will find it profitable to browse through the pages and reflect upon the chapter titles and recall the events.

As you must have discovered, it is fun to talk over books with others. Many of the happenings in *The Human Comedy* may recall experiences to you and impel you to talk of them and to write.

In all probability Mr. Saroyan would say, "Write! Don't pause to ask whether the result will be poem, essay, story, play, or novel. Write!"

DON FREEMAN'S SKETCHES

The small boy and the Negro waved to one another until the train was almost out of sight.

Are Mr. Freeman's sketches dramatic? frivolous? Has the artist caught the mood of the story? What details are significant?

Don Freeman, a native of San Diego, California, loves the theater. Inspired by *Penrod,* he staged amateur theatricals in a garage. At nineteen he viewed New York with wonder and remained, studying art under John Sloan and Harry Wickey, and playing a trumpet to make a living. He helped to create the part of Harold and to act it in Mr. Saroyan's *The Beautiful People,* which ran in New York in 1941 for one hundred and twenty performances.

Look up Mr. Freeman. Bring pictures to class. You will find material in *Art News,* vol. 38, page 18, February, 1940; *Magazine of Art,* vol. 33, page 175, March, 1940; *Newsweek,* vol. 15, page 35, Feb. 19, 1940; the *Christian Science Monitor Magazine,* Oct. 10, 1942; and the New York *Times Magazine,* Feb. 28, 1943.

If you like to draw, make some line sketches for an original paper. Try to sketch for the school newspaper or magazine.

MUSIC IN *THE HUMAN COMEDY*
*He burst out with a shouting of music —
simple, lyrical and ridiculous.*

Grand operas or symphonies were not essential in the life of the Macauleys and their friends, but rather songs such as "My Old Kentucky Home" and "O Sole Mio"; hymns such as "Rock of Ages," "Leaning on the Everlasting Arms," and "Let There Be Light"; and the spontaneous singing of soldiers. There are the organ in church, the piano and the harp in Ulysses's home, the pianola in Corbett's, the accordion Marcus took to war and the beautiful music that Spangler found in telegraph keys: "real music—straight from the world—straight from the hearts of people."

A Philosophy of Life

If songs form any part of your memories, give lines from them.

THE SCENE OF *THE HUMAN COMEDY*
When are we going home?

You read of Matthew; Marcus; Homer, Ulysses, Diana, and Ithaca; the Beaufreres; Mr. Ara; of gopher holes; of cactus candy; of walnut, china-ball, fig, olive, pomegranate, persimmon, mariposa, and apricot trees; of vineyards; and of the Santa Fé Railway.

What is the scene of the novel: California, nowhere, everywhere?

MR. SAROYAN'S PHILOSOPHY OF LIFE
Look at that! Homer kept saying to himself of earth and tree, sun and grass and cloud.

Saroyan's characters stop to tell what they value. Their admissions, which might easily seem preachy, frequently focus attention on things too often taken for granted. Perhaps because of his foreign ancestry Saroyan views with wonder and delight, even with rhapsody, important things which many natives fail to perceive.

In the story of Homer is a concern for elemental things: love, work, war, loneliness, pity, and death— things mysterious and baffling to adults as to younger people. Homer and Ulysses don't understand about death. Neither did the child in Wordsworth's poem, for she insisted "We are seven."

The Human Comedy

You read that the world is transfigured by one who loves people, that you should give of everything you have, and that you should try to love everyone you meet. Are those sound ideas?

Homer says his job makes school seem silly. Is his mother right when she replies, "Schools are only to keep children off the street; sooner or later they get there"?

Would you like to treat mistakes "as wonderful mistakes that you must and will make" and must not be afraid of making?

Important and prosaic things are linked. Mr. Grogan weaves in the fact that the accumulating of money is most unimportant; he goes right on, "It's a night letter." He concludes comments on immortality by asking, "Are you any good at pitching horseshoes?"

What, if anyone or anything, does Mr. Saroyan criticize? Does he take a superior attitude? Is his outlook on life bitter or kindly?

DEMOCRACY IN *THE HUMAN COMEDY*
" Blessed are the humble, for they shall see God."

What could be more democratic than the incident in the first chapter in which Ulysses waves at the Negro on the train that is passing? Of what are the tiny boy, the Negro on the gondola, the singing of "My Old Kentucky home," and the waving of hands a symbol?

Our idea of democracy is said to have come from the Bible. *The Human Comedy* has been called a commentary on the Bible. What is the connection between the lesson in ancient history and the Bible? Read as a verse choir the passages from the Scriptures on pages 253–254.

Wordsworth ushered in a literary era with *Lyrical Ballads,* which included "The Mad Mother," "The Idiot Boy," and "The Convict." Saroyan has written of Charley and of Lionel Cabot, a generous and sweet-tempered half-wit. What is the democratic attitude toward such people?

America has been a melting pot. In what way does Mr. Ara help to illustrate this? Do the picnics in the chapter about the trees and the vines also illustrate America as a melting pot?

Oftentimes tolerance is talked of but not practised. In the story where does there seem to be genuine tolerance? Was there true democracy in the high school in Ithaca? Is there true democracy in your high school?

THE HUMAN COMEDY AND THE WAR

The three soldiers began leaping over one another at a swift, crazy game of leapfrog, pushing down the dark, immortal street nearer and nearer to the War.

The impact of the war is felt through telegrams and letters, homes changed by absent ones, work problems, Marcus and Tobey, and by attempts to penetrate the complex happening called war.

As issues in connection with the making of peace, you might think of Mr. Grogan's explanation of war, ᴜne body of the world fighting off its diseases. Optimistically he believes "the sick body and the sick spirit are always restored to health." The soldier called Fat tells that "we are of one family, the human, and except for the war we might never meet." Marcus, a soldier, cannot recognize a human being as his enemy; he says, "My quarrel is not with *him* but with that in him which I seek to destroy in myself first."

What do you think of the description of the service men in the first paragraph of Chapter 31? Relate the story of a service man you know, comparing him with Marcus or Tobey George.

THE HUMAN COMEDY AS A NOVEL

The pattern of life in Ithaca — of people everywhere in the world — followed a design which at first seemed senseless and crazy, but as the days and nights gathered together as months and years, the pattern was seen to have had beauty of form.

And so it is in a way with *The Human Comedy*. At first the book may seem to lack pattern; it may then emerge for you with beauty of form.

It is difficult to define a novel. The word means many different things. Most critics agree that a novel should have some kind of design. Pattern, however, is not nearly so important as life: the book should be throbbing and alive. Julian Green, a novelist, said it is hard for a writer to give the sound of a beating heart unless he is alive and unless like Dickens he remembers something of his childhood. A great novelist will describe a tree as if he had never seen one before and make the reader share the experience. Mr. Saroyan has a sense of form. He is alive and views with wonder an egg, a tree, an apricot.

Mr. Green compared a novel to an iceberg with one third above sea level and two thirds below; one third expressed and two thirds in indivisible depths. Much of *The Human Comedy* has not been expressed; for that reason it is more powerful. Some of the submerged is revealed in plays and stories by Mr. Saroyan; for example, "Seventy Thousand Assyrians," "School," "Fifty-Yard Dash," "Pomegranate Trees," "Five Ripe Pears," and "Presbyterian Choir Singers."

Details and incidents are not haphazard but deliberate. Chapters are connected. Matthew foreshadows for Katey the fact that Marcus is going to come with him.

Does Mr. Saroyan succeed in "translating into lucid expression straight from the normally unlucid and disjointed pages of human experience"? He said that that translation is no easy thing to do.

MR. SAROYAN'S IDEAS

In reflecting upon *The Human Comedy* you might like to consider some of the ideas that Mr. Saroyan expressed in earlier writing. Has he followed his own advice?

The Human Comedy

I am about to place language, my language, upon a clean sheet of paper, and I am trembling. It is so much of a responsibility to be a user of words.—"Myself upon the Earth" [1]

I am a story-teller, and I have but a single story—man. I want to tell this simple story in my own way, forgetting the rules of rhetoric, the tricks of composition. I have something to say and I do not wish to speak like Balzac. I am not an artist; I do not really believe in civilization. I am not at all enthusiastic about progress. When a great bridge is built I do not cheer, and when airplanes cross the Atlantic I do not think, "What a marvelous age this is!" I am not interested in the destiny of nations, and history bores me. What do they mean by history, those who write it and believe in it?—"Myself upon the Earth"

I do not believe in transportation, in going places with the body, and I would like to know where anyone has ever gone. Have you ever left yourself? Is any journey so vast and interesting as the journey of the mind through life? Is the end of any journey so beautiful as death?—"Myself upon the Earth"

The thing to remember, always, is to encourage naturalness, lucidity, simplicity, ease, and good humor: these are American qualities.—Note for *Narration with a Red Piano* [2]

Don't let form (the mechanics: techniques and so on) hinder anybody. If a man says twenty words that are fresh and genuine, these words are *themselves form*. Don't let,

[1] Passages from "Myself upon the Earth" are reprinted from *The Daring Young Man on the Flying Trapeze* with the kind permission of Random House.

[2] Passages from "Note," by William Saroyan, for *Narration with a Red Piano*, by J. Calder Joseph, edited and arranged by Robert J. Lowry, are reprinted with the kind permission of The Little Man Press.

Mr. Saroyan's Ideas

I mean, words like poem, short story, essay, and so on, hinder anybody from speaking.—Note for *Narration with a Red Piano*

The ambition to have is one that stays at home, within each man: to grow, to be balanced (that means proportion, fullness, wholeness as, for instance, we know Shakespeare to be balanced), and to learn how to translate into lucid expression straight from the normally unlucid and disjointed page of human experience. That is no easy thing to do. The source, that is, must be the man himself, and not other writing. What I'm trying to say is, first try for *living* writing. Make the language plain, unliterary, direct, unaffected, easy-going; that won't keep the writer from being great, if *he* is great; it will, on the contrary, help him. One thing more, only: don't be supercilious (even unconsciously) toward people who cannot write, who don't like to read, who seem to be dumb, who *are* perhaps dumb; unfriendliness toward others is ultimately only poor understanding of one's self. The dumbest, dullest, dopiest, dizziest, vulgarest, most insignificant, meanest, unfriendliest man in the world is a variation of myself; as the noblest, finest, truest man is too.—Note for *Narration with a Red Piano*

In the time of your life, live—so that in that good time there shall be no ugliness or death for yourself or for any life your life touches. Seek goodness everywhere, and when it is found, bring it out of its hiding-place and let it be free and unashamed. Place in matter and in flesh the least of the values, for these are the things that hold death and must pass away. Discover in all things that which shines and is beyond corruption.—*The Time of Your Life* [1]

---

[1] The passage from Saroyan's *The Time of Your Life* is reprinted with the kind permission of Harcourt, Brace and Company.

The Human Comedy

YOUR NEXT READING

"You can't know what a book says, Ulysses, unless you can read."

It is not necessary for you to read other books in connection with *The Human Comedy,* but if you *can* read, you might like to.

So many have wondered about the use of the word *comedy* that perhaps you should read some famous comedies and make up your own mind about comedy.

Dante's *Divine Comedy*
(Anonymous) *Master Pierre Patelin*
Cervantes' *Don Quixote*
Shakespeare's *The Comedy of Errors*
Molière's *The Miser*
Sheridan's *The Rivals*
Goldsmith's *She Stoops to Conquer*
Meredith's *The Egoist*
Barrie's *The Admirable Crichton*
Galsworthy's *The Silver Box*
Galsworthy's *A Modern Comedy*

Sometimes people refer to these authors in relation to William Saroyan. Why do you suppose they do so?

Sherwood Anderson, " What Makes a Boy Afraid," *Modern Short Stories,* Reppert

Ernest Hemingway, " Cat in the Rain," *International Short Stories,* Church

Ring Lardner, " Alibi Ike," *Modern Short Stories,* Reppert

Thornton Wilder, *The Bridge of San Luis Rey*

Thornton Wilder, *Our Town*

Since Mr. Saroyan is a contemporary and has written so many things, you will find many magazine references in the *Readers' Guide.* At any rate look in *Life,* volume 9, pages 96–100, November 18, 1940.

Your Next Reading

Read a poem by Mr. Saroyan, "Saroyan Prizes: 1900–1940," in the *New Yorker*, vol. 16, page 14, Aug. 31, 1940. Copies of *Scholastic* should be helpful.

Though these books differ in many ways, there is a special bond between each one and *The Human Comedy.*

Barrie's *Margaret Ogilvie*
Cather's *My Antonia*
Day's *Life With Father*
Dickens' *David Copperfield*
Dickens' *Great Expectations*
Dickens' *Oliver Twist*
Ferber's *American Beauty*
Grahame's *The Wind in the Willows*

Kipling's *Kim*
Rawlings's *The Yearling*
Swift's *Gulliver's Travels*
Tarkington's *Penrod*
Thoreau's "Conclusions," *Walden*
Twain's *The Adventures of Huckleberry Finn*
Walpole's *Jeremy*

B B
C C
D D 8
E E 9
F F 0
G G 1
H H 2
I I 3
J J 4